MEDITERR...

Let these exotic doc...

Be tantalised by th...
romanced by their fiery passion,
and warmed by the emotional power
of these strong and caring men...

MEDITERRANEAN DOCTORS

Passionate about life, love and medicine.

'Papa.'

Matteo's voice cut through the maelstrom of emotions whirling around inside him and Luca jumped.

Turning, Luca realised Kelly was standing, stock still, in the middle of the driveway.

'Whose house is this?' Her voice was so low that it sounded as though all the life had seeped out of it, and his fear intensified.

'Mine,' he said simply. 'This is where I live.'

Her eyes closed for a moment, before she opened them again and stared at him. 'If this is your house, then who is Matteo? Where are his parents?'

He had promised Sophia that he would never tell anyone the truth about Matteo's birth and he never had. Matteo was his son, and that was what everyone must continue to believe. Including Kelly…especially Kelly.

'Matteo is my son, Kelly.'

DR FERRERO'S BABY SECRET

BY
JENNIFER TAYLOR

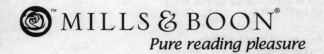

MILLS & BOON®
Pure reading pleasure

First published in Great Britain 2007
Harlequin Mills & Boon Limited,
Eton House, 18-24 Paradise Road, Richmond, Surrey TW9 1SR

© Jennifer Taylor 2007

ISBN-13: 978 0 263 85263 9

Set in Times Roman 10½ on 12½ pt
03-0907-50595

Printed and bound in Spain
by Litografia Rosés, S.A., Barcelona

DR FERRERO'S
BABY SECRET

Dear Reader

My husband and I love to travel, so when I came up with the idea of writing two books about twin sisters it seemed the perfect opportunity to use two of our very favourite places as settings for the stories. Bill and I spent our honeymoon in Sardinia, so that had to be one of the places I chose, and then last year we went to Cyprus for our wedding anniversary and had a wonderful time there, so I chose that as the second location. We've had great fun looking through all the photographs together.

Katie and Kelly Carlyon have a lot in common, apart from being twins. They both work in the world of medicine, and they have both fallen in love with men who live in the Mediterranean. Whilst Katie flies to Cyprus to be with the man she loves, Kelly moves to Sardinia to forget about the man who has broken her heart. However, as they soon discover, life doesn't always work out the way you hope it will!

I really enjoyed writing the two books in this mini-series, and hope that if you liked reading Katie's story in DR CONSTANTINE'S BRIDE you will enjoy Kelly's story here in DR FERRERO'S BABY SECRET too.

Love

Jennifer

www.jennifer-taylor.com

CHAPTER ONE

SHE had made her decision. She would hand in her notice and leave at the end of the week. She had spent the night thinking about it and realised it was the only rational solution. Getting this job might have been the fulfilment of all her dreams, but no job was worth this amount of heartache.

Kelly Carlyon felt her heart start to pound when she heard the office door open. She knew what she *should* do, yet the irrational part of her couldn't bear to think that Luca might believe she was too scared to work with him. She had got over him a long time ago, as soon as she had found out that he was going to marry another woman, in fact.

Admittedly, it had been a shock when she had arrived at the hospital to take up the post of junior registrar and discovered that he was her new boss, but she had made up her mind that she would deal with the situation professionally. However, after the argument they'd had yesterday, she was less confident of that. Could she really work with Luca Ferrero when there was so much history between them?

'*Buongiorno,* Kelly.'

Luca swept into the office and closed the door. Kelly felt a wave of resentment rise up inside her as she watched him walk over to his desk. There was no sign of discomfort on his handsome face, no hint at all that he found the situation as stressful as she did. Luca didn't give a damn that he had turned her world upside down again. If he had cared then he would never have treated her the way he'd done two years ago.

Kelly's mouth compressed as she recalled what had happened. Luca had spent six months as visiting consultant on the paediatric unit where she'd been working as a senior house officer and that was how they had met. The intensity of her feelings for him had taken her completely by surprise. She'd been too busy establishing her career to get romantically involved with anyone, yet within a week of them meeting she and Luca had been lovers.

She'd been devastated when he'd returned to Rome at the end of his tenure. Even though he had sworn that they would always be together, she'd been so afraid of losing him. When he had telephoned her a week later to say that he was back in England and needed to see her, she had been elated. She had rushed home after work, sure in her own mind that he was going to ask her to go back to Italy with him, but she'd been wrong.

When Luca had arrived, he had refused her invitation to sit down. He had stood in the middle of her living room and had told her simply that he was getting married. Oh, he had tried to break it to her gently, said that he had never meant to hurt her, but she had stopped listening. The truth was that she had served her purpose and he'd had no further use for her.

She had ordered him to leave and that had been the last she'd seen of him until she'd arrived in Sardinia. Now, as the newly appointed head of clinical care at the Santa Margherita

Ospedale, a hospital devoted to the care of sick children on Sardinia's northern coast, Luca must be more determined than ever that she wasn't going to stand in his way.

'So, Kelly, have you decided what you intend to do?'

Luca pulled out a chair and sat down. Kelly took a deep breath as she blanked out the unhappy memories. Luca had given her twenty-four hours to decide if she wanted to continue working at the hospital and he wouldn't allow her a second more. She opened her mouth to tell him that she had decided to leave when he interrupted her.

'Before you say anything, I believe I owe you an apology.'

'An apology?' she repeated uncertainly.

'*Si.*' He leant back in his chair and studied her across the width of the desk. 'It was wrong of me to speak to you that way in front of the team. I apologise for it.'

'Oh! I see.'

Kelly bit her lip, hoping he couldn't tell how emotional she felt. She'd been bitterly upset by what had happened yesterday. Luca had been extremely abrupt with her when she had suggested a change of treatment for one of the children. It wouldn't have been so bad if he had taken the time to consider her idea, but he had dismissed it out of hand. She had been furious about the way he had spoken to her and had told him so in no uncertain terms. If he hadn't been called away, she knew that a full-scale row would have erupted and that would have been reprehensible. It was bad enough that Luca had felt it necessary to advise her to consider her position at the hospital before he had left. Maybe Luca wasn't the only one who needed to apologise?

'I think I owe you an apology too. I should have accepted what you said and not argued with you.'

'Then we were both at fault, it seems.'

He shrugged, his broad shoulders moving lightly beneath his suit jacket. He was always impeccably dressed and the black suit he was wearing fitted him like a glove, moulding itself to the lean lines of his body. He had chosen a plain white shirt to go with it and the colour was the perfect foil for the olive tan of his skin. With those deep grey eyes and that lustrous black hair, he looked more like a film star than a doctor, yet it hadn't just been his looks that had attracted her when they had met. It had been everything about him: his vitality; his commitment; his intelligence. Luca Ferrero had seemed like the embodiment of all her dreams and it was little wonder that she had fallen in love with him. The hardest thing of all had been discovering that her idol had clay feet.

It was painful to recall again what had happened so she pushed the memory to the back of her mind. It wasn't relevant now, anyway. The days when she and Luca had been lovers were long gone and a lot had happened since, her move to Sardinia to work at the Santa Margherita hospital being one of the major events.

Moving abroad had been a big step for her and her twin sister, Katie. When she had moved to Sardinia, Katie had gone to live in Cyprus. Kelly had been worried in case things didn't work out for her twin but, after speaking to Katie the previous night, and discovering that she was getting married, Kelly was confident the move had been a success for one of them at least. It was one less thing to worry about if she had to give up her job here.

Kelly frowned when she realised that an element of doubt had crept into her mind. She had decided that she must leave and that should have been the end of it. However, part of her was still reluctant to give up the job and life she had dreamed about for so long.

'So, Kelly, you were about to tell me what you have decided to do.'

Kelly felt panic well up inside her again as Luca prompted her for an answer. All of a sudden she wasn't sure what she was going to tell him. Should she hand in her notice, or should she stay? But if she stayed, she was going to have to work with him on a daily basis. Could she treat him as just another colleague, or would the memory of the past always affect her judgement, as it had done yesterday? She had never argued with someone senior to her before, yet she'd had no compunction when it had come to squaring up to Luca.

'I know how difficult this is for you, Kelly. It's not easy for me, either.'

Luca's tone had softened, stroking along her raw nerves like a velvet-gloved hand, and she shivered. She had always been highly responsive to him. Just a word or a touch and she'd been like putty in his hands. That was another reason why she should leave—she didn't want to feel like that again. Luca was a married man now and he was strictly off limits. However, even though she knew that, she couldn't help the feelings that were trickling through her, hot little shivers which she hated yet couldn't control.

'I can't see why it should upset you, Luca,' she said sharply, trying to quell the treacherous response of her body. 'You forgot all about me the moment you left England. After all, you had other things on your mind, didn't you?'

'If you mean that my life changed dramatically after I returned to Italy, I won't deny it,' he said quietly. 'However, it doesn't mean that I forgot what we shared while I was in

England. You played a very important role in my life during the time I was there, Kelly, so this situation is just as difficult for me as it is for you. However, we're both adults and I honestly believe that we can find a way to work together if we put our minds to it.'

'Does that mean you want me to stay on here?' she asked in surprise because she had never expected him to make such an admission. Luca had been cool to the point of indifference since she'd arrived. He'd given no hint that he remembered the time they had spent together. Although it shouldn't have made a scrap of difference to discover that he considered her an important part of his past, she knew that it did.

'Yes. But only if it's what you want, too.' He leant forward and his eyes were very intent all of a sudden. 'I won't try to persuade you to do something you don't feel is right for you, Kelly. I have too much respect for you both as a person and as a doctor.'

'Thank you.' Kelly took a quick breath when she felt her emotions see-saw once more. 'I would like to stay. It's always been my dream to work in a children's hospital. I couldn't believe it when I was told that I had the job.'

'Me, too.' A sudden smile curled his sensual mouth as he leant back in his chair. 'I knew there were dozens of candidates for the post and that they came from all over the world, too. I could scarcely believe my good fortune when the board offered me the job of clinical director.'

'Stop being so modest.' Kelly smiled back, feeling some of her tension ease when she saw the laughter on his face. This was the Luca she remembered best, the warm, caring man who took such delight in even the smallest success. No wonder everyone had adored him when he'd worked in

Manchester. He could have had his pick of all the single women in the hospital, but he'd chosen her.

The thought sent a frisson scudding through her but she ignored it. She laughed, wanting to keep the mood light because it was safer. 'You know very well there are few paediatricians who can match you, Luca.'

'Hmm, I think I should hire you to do my PR. You are very good for my ego, Kelly.'

He returned her smile before he abruptly sobered. She had the impression that he was deliberately drawing back and couldn't help feeling disappointed before she realised how stupid it was. She should be glad that he was keen to keep their relationship on a strictly platonic footing.

'You are an excellent doctor, Kelly. The proof of that is the fact that the board offered you this job. Whilst I hadn't taken up my own post when you were interviewed, I wouldn't have had any hesitation about endorsing your application if I'd been consulted.'

'Thank you. That means a lot to me. I thought… Well, you can probably guess what I thought.'

'That if I'd had the chance I would have found a way to stop you working here?' He sighed. 'It's speculation at this stage, but I'd like to think that I would have considered your application on its own merits. You have a very promising career ahead of you, Kelly. That was obvious when we worked together in Manchester. I know how committed you are and I wouldn't want to do anything that would prevent you achieving your potential.'

There was something about the way he said it that bothered her. Kelly had a feeling that her career really mattered to him and that he wasn't just saying so for appearances' sake.

However, before she could reply, the phone rang. She waited while Luca took the call. It was obviously bad news because he looked grim when he hung up.

'Alessandro Alessi—the boy we saw yesterday during ward rounds—has suffered a convulsion. I'll make my way straight to the ward. Can you tell the rest of the team to meet me there, please?'

'Of course.'

Kelly stood up as he came around the desk. She followed him out of the office but soon got left behind. She headed for the staff lounge and relayed the message, trying to ignore the speculation on everyone's faces as they made their way to the ward. They were obviously wondering if she was going to stay after what had happened yesterday so should she tell them that she had decided to leave, or should she wait until she was sure it was what she really wanted to do?

She pushed open the ward door and felt her heart scrunch up inside her when she saw Luca talking to the sister. Whether she stayed or went, it was going to hurt and there was no point pretending otherwise.

'Grazie.'

Luca handed the chart to the sister and walked over to the bed. Ten-year-old Alessandro had been admitted with a severe headache and fever ten days earlier. Luca had immediately suspected bacterial meningitis and had had him rushed to the intensive care unit without waiting to do a lumbar puncture to confirm his diagnosis first. By the time the characteristic rash had appeared a short time later, Alessandro had been receiving intravenous antibiotics, and they had undoubtedly saved his life. That the child should have suffered this setback now was a blow.

'How long did the convulsion last?' he asked, his gaze centred on the boy. He knew that his team was gathering around him but he didn't look up because he didn't want anything to distract him…

His pulse leapt when someone brushed past him. He didn't need to look to know it was Kelly. His internal radar had been working overtime since she had arrived. He could pinpoint her position in a room with complete accuracy, and the thought troubled him deeply.

He couldn't afford to feel like this—it wasn't fair to Kelly or to himself. He had promised Sophia that he would love and care for Matteo for the rest of his life, and that's what he was going to do. There was no room in his life for anyone except his son, and he certainly didn't intend to jeopardise Kelly's career prospects by involving her in his affairs.

'How long did the seizure last?' he reiterated, clearing his mind of everything else.

'Only a few minutes,' Sister replied. 'One of the junior nurses alerted me. By the time I got here, Alessandro was fine, but I thought I should let you know immediately, *dottore*.'

'You did exactly the right thing. I want to know about any changes that occur as soon as they happen,' Luca said firmly, wondering how long it would take him to drum that into his staff. Some of the nurses in particular were loath to call him in case it appeared they couldn't cope. However, he didn't care how many false alarms he was called to if it meant a tragedy could be averted.

He smiled at the boy. 'So how do you feel now, Alessandro?'

'All right, I guess,' Alessandro muttered.

'*Bene.*' Luca nodded, although he could tell that the child wasn't as alert as he'd been the last time he'd seen him. Taking a pen torch out of his pocket, he checked the boy's response to light. If he wasn't mistaken, the right eye hadn't reacted as quickly as it should have done. The delay was infinitesimal but enough to make him decide that he would value a second opinion.

He glanced around the group, pleased to see that everyone was present. He'd made it clear when he had taken over that he expected them to turn up on time for ward rounds. The team had grown a little lax after his predecessor had left but Luca wasn't prepared to accept less than one hundred per cent commitment from every single one of them. His gaze skimmed over his senior registrar, Carlo Baldovini, an earnest young man in his thirties. Next to Carlo was Letizia Sentini, one of the two junior registrars on the team. Letizia smiled at him, although he didn't respond. He wasn't interested in Letizia's less than subtle attempts to flirt with him.

His gaze came to rest on Kelly and he felt a sudden tightening in his chest. He knew how difficult it was going to be to keep their relationship on a professional footing if she stayed at the hospital. Of all the women he had known, Kelly was the one who had touched him most. When he'd met Kelly, he'd found his soul mate, but once Sophia had told him about the baby she was expecting, he had realised that he would have to let Kelly go.

He knew that if he had to make the decision again, he would do exactly the same thing. However, as he looked at Kelly's face, he couldn't help wishing that circumstances had been different. If he'd not had to care for Sophia and her unborn child, he and Kelly might still be together.

'It is one option,' Luca agreed
and raised his brows. 'Do y
Should we opt for surger
'I don't think it's
Kelly replied, ign
gave her. Sh
deterred
prov

18

'THERE'S a hint of sl
reacts.'

Kelly carefully eras... ...ion from her face as she turned to Luca. She had... ...pected him to solicit her opinion after what had happened yesterday, although she wasn't going to let him know that.

'*Si.* That is what I thought as well.'

He took the light from her and bent over the child once more. Kelly breathed a sigh of relief. At least it appeared they agreed on something and that had to be a step in the right direction. If they could carry on this way then she might be able to stay on here.

Her heart gave a little flutter at the thought but she damped it down. She wasn't going to rush into making a decision now it appeared that Luca had given her a stay of execution. She glanced round in surprise when Letizia suddenly stepped forward and rudely elbowed her aside.

'Perhaps there is a blockage,' the registrar suggested as she took Kelly's place. 'If an excess of cerebrospinal fluid has been collecting inside the skull, it could have caused the child to have a seizure. We shall need to operate to relieve the pressure.'

almly. He looked at Kelly ou agree with Letizia, Kelly?

ossible to say for certain at this stage,' oring the venomous look the other woman directed her answer to Luca, refusing to be from making her point. 'It will need a CT scan to if there is a blockage or not.'

'Indeed it will, which is why we should not be too hasty.' Luca glanced at Letizia. 'If you could arrange for Alessandro to have a CT scan we shall decide how to proceed once we have seen the results.' He shrugged. 'It could be that there is infection still present so we need to check on that, too.'

'You wish to do a lumbar puncture?' Letizia suggested immediately.

'No. A lumbar puncture should never be performed if there is a chance that intracranial pressure has been raised,' he said reprovingly. 'Blood tests will suffice for now.'

He moved away from the bed, indicating that he needed a word with the ward sister. Kelly followed the group as they all trooped to the next bed. Letizia gave her a look of loathing as she swept past her and went to the phone. Kelly sighed. She had a nasty feeling that she had made herself an enemy even though she had never intended to do so. Still, she could hardly have gone along with Letizia's suggestion when she hadn't agreed with her.

The rest of the round passed smoothly, although Kelly took care to keep out of Letizia's way. There was a morning clinic after it was over so she made her way to the outpatients department on the ground floor. Aldo, one of the cleaners, was mopping up some orange juice which had been spilled on the floor and he paused to speak to her. He was learning English and loved to practise whenever he had the chance.

'It is a beautiful day, *dottoressa,*' he said, smiling shyly at her.

'*Si, Aldo, molto bello,*' Kelly replied. She knew from her own experience of learning Italian how important it was to practice and was more than happy to help. She left him to get on with his work and carried on to the office. Serafina, one of the reception staff, smiled when Kelly went in.

'*Buongiorno,* Kelly. You have a long list today, I'm afraid. There are several children whom Dr Ferrero asked specifically to see as well so do you know if he will be along soon?'

'He shouldn't be long now,' Kelly assured her, picking up the list. As Serafina had said, it was a long list and she doubted if she would be finished in time for lunch, not that it worried her if she had to work through her break. Her patients came first and they always would.

She put the list back on the desk and picked up the stack of files the receptionist had prepared for her. 'I'll make a start,' she began, then glanced round when the door opened as Luca arrived. He reached past her and picked up the list, and Kelly felt her breath lock in her throat when his arm brushed her shoulder. She couldn't seem to breathe so that it was left to him to speak.

'There is a case I would like to discuss with you, Kelly.' He glanced at her and she realised that he had no inkling what was happening to her. His tone was perfectly level when he continued and contrarily she couldn't help the feeling of disappointment that swept through her. 'It will be easier if we do it after clinic is over so come to my office when you have finished your list.'

He didn't wait for her to reply before he left—didn't need to, either. He was in charge and she was there to carry out his instructions. However, as the door closed behind him, Kelly knew that their working relationship had nothing to do with the way she was feeling right then.

She hurriedly left the office and went to the consulting room the registrars used. A plastic strip bearing her name had been slotted into place on the door and she stopped to look at it, needing to remind herself who she was: Dr Kelly Carlyon. Junior Registrar. Clinical Care.

She was a member of Luca's team now and nothing more. She had to forget that he was the man she had loved with all her heart if she intended to stay here. There must be no more looking back at the past, and definitely no repeat of what had happened just now.

Heat suffused her as she recalled the way his arm had brushed against her. It had been the most fleeting contact yet she could feel her skin tingling as it had always done whenever Luca had touched her. Luca had been the most wonderful lover. She'd had little experience when they had met, but he had taught her to how to give love and how to receive it as well. She had come alive in his arms, but she mustn't make the mistake of thinking it could happen again. Luca was a married man now and even if she stayed, he could never make her feel like that again.

A sob rose in her throat as she hurriedly entered the office but she forced it down. Dropping the files onto the desk, she took off her jacket and put on a clean white coat. She smoothed down the collar then checked her appearance in the mirror over the handbasin, wanting to be sure that everything was in order before her patients arrived.

Her dark red hair was neatly coiled at the nape of her neck in the style she favoured for work. She'd decided to wear a touch of make-up that morning to bolster her courage and the slick of lip gloss and coat of mascara added to the overall picture of a woman in control of her life. On the outside, at least, she looked much the same as she always did. It was only her eyes that betrayed her inner turbulence.

Pain lanced through her as she studied the shadows that clouded their sea-green depths. The fact that Luca had been completely unmoved when they'd touched just now hurt unbearably. Once, she would have confidently claimed that he'd loved her as much as she had loved him, but she'd been wrong. Luca hadn't loved her then and he most certainly didn't love her now.

'Come in.'

Luca steeled himself as the door opened but it was only Serafina with some messages for him. He thanked her, shaking his head when she asked him if he wanted a cup of coffee. 'No. *Grazie.*'

He managed to hold his smile until she left but the tension was starting to tell on him. All morning long he had tried to forget how it had felt when he had brushed against Kelly but he'd failed. He could still feel it deep inside him—her softly yielding flesh, her smooth firm skin, her heat.

He swore softly, fluently, using the language he had learned as a child growing up in one of the poorest parts of Italy. The people in charge of the children's home where he had been sent to live had called it gutter language and had washed out his mouth with soap and water, but even that hadn't stopped him. It had been the only way he had been able to release the pain and anger that burned inside him.

It hadn't been until he had finished his degree that he had taught himself not to say the ugly words out loud. The anger had still been there, of course, along with the painful memories of his childhood. It had only been when he had met Kelly that they had started to fade. She'd made him see that he was no longer that ragged, unkempt urchin but a man whom a woman could love. The man Kelly had loved.

How it hurt to know that he could have had a lifetime of her love if things had been different. It wasn't that he had thrown it heedlessly away—he'd had no choice. Sophia had needed him and he couldn't have lived with himself if he had abandoned her and her unborn child. He had traded one kind of love for another and he didn't regret his decision. He had loved Kelly with all his heart, but she hadn't *needed* him like Sophia had done.

Luca jumped when there was a second knock on the door. 'Come in,' he called, picking up the bundle of messages so it would appear as though he had been doing something useful instead of sitting there, daydreaming.

He heard the door open and footsteps cross the room but he didn't look up. He didn't need to. He knew it was Kelly, he could smell her scent, hear her breathing, feel her presence in every fibre of his being. He allowed himself a single, glorious second to savour the sensations that washed through him then banished them to where those memories resided. He had indulged himself enough for one day.

'How was clinic?' His tone was cool, distant, polite, the voice he used with all his staff. Luca Ferrero, the physician, gave away nothing about himself, neither the man he was today nor the child he had been. He didn't fraternise with his colleagues because he didn't have the time. Every second of every day was devoted either to his work or his son and that's how he intended it to continue, especially now that Kelly was here. Kelly was the one person who could make him question the path he had chosen, the only one who could make him want more than he had.

'Fine. Most of the children were follow-up cases so there were no problems.'

'*Bene.*' He glanced up at last, felt his heart lurch, and swiftly recovered. So maybe she was standing in a patch of sunlight that was setting her glorious hair alight but it made no difference to him. He was centred, focused wholly and exclusively on his job.

She shifted slightly and his heart jolted again as he watched her slender body move beneath the white coat. He knew that he would never actually do it, but he longed to get up and walk around the desk, unbutton that coat and peel it off her then set to work on that prim little blouse which she wore underneath.

His vision blurred as he pictured his hands moving down the row of tiny pearl buttons until the very last one had been unfastened. He knew from experience that her skin would be barely darker than the fabric—milky-pale, smooth, unblemished—and shuddered. He would slowly open her blouse, breathe in her scent, feel the warmth of her skin, pull her to him and…

'You said that you wanted to discuss a case with me.'

Her voice was sharp; it cut through the image that was playing in his head with rapier-like speed so that he almost gasped out loud. He managed to quash the sound before it emerged, but it shook him to know how close he had come to disaster. What the hell was he doing, playing such dangerous mind games?

'That's right.' He stood up and went to the filing cabinet, waving her to a chair as though he didn't care where she sat or what she did. It wasn't true because he cared a lot, cared deeply about whether she was going to stay or leave, and how much time he could spend with her.

He slammed the drawer, wishing he could lock his thoughts away as easily. 'The patient's name is Domenico del Pietro, a fifteen-year-old boy who lives in Palau with his parents.' He handed her the file and sat down. 'He was referred to us following a number of consultations with his own doctor.'

Kelly frowned as she read through the case history. 'Fever, headache, muscle pain, tenderness, nausea. A general feeling of tiredness and malaise.' She looked up. 'There's nothing here about his mental state. How did he appear when you saw him?'

'Somewhat depressed,' Luca replied, inwardly smiling. It seemed that Kelly was already thinking along the right lines, not that he was surprised. She'd always been extremely sharp, quick to diagnose and accurate, too, which was more important. He carried on feeding her information, wondering how long it would take her to reach the same conclusion he had arrived at. 'His teachers have also noticed a definite loss of concentration in recent months. Domenico is usually an A-grade student but his work has suffered of late.'

'Any panic attacks or sleep disturbance?'

'None reported.'

'Has a full neurological assessment been carried out?'

'Not yet. Domenico is due to come into hospital tomorrow and we shall do it then.'

'I imagine you've ruled out mononucleosis. He's the right age for it so it must have been your first thought.'

'It was, but the tests came back negative.' He leant back in his chair. 'So, Kelly, have you any suggestions?'

'ME.' She placed the file on the desk. 'The symptoms are all indicative of myalgic encephalomyelitis.'

'And you ascribe to the school of thought that says ME is an actual illness and not the result of a psychiatric disorder like depression?'

'Yes, I do.' She met his gaze across the desk. 'I don't doubt that anyone who suffers from ME also suffers from depression—who wouldn't when you're feeling ill all the time? However, I'm convinced there is a physical cause for it. Most people who present with symptoms of ME have had a viral infection, haven't they?'

'Domenico had an upper-respiratory tract infection six months ago.'

'And it was after that his symptoms appeared?' she said.

'*Si,*' Luca agreed, enjoying watching her piecing together the puzzle.

She nodded as she picked up the file and glanced at the lab results. 'Recent tests show everything is normal, which is what I would have expected. It's rare that the lab comes up with anything in a case of ME.'

'It is. So what do you recommend?'

'That we wait for the results of the neurological tests and go from there,' she said promptly.

'Which is exactly what I have decided to do.' Luca smiled, unable to hide his satisfaction. It was good to know that his faith in her hadn't been misplaced. 'Maybe you would like to be involved in this case, Kelly. It will be good experience for you to follow the boy's progress.'

'I'd like that. Thank you.' She briefly returned his smile then stood up. 'If that's all, I'd better get back. We overran this morning and Serafina has rebooked a couple of cases for this afternoon. I want to read through their notes before I see them.'

Luca frowned as he checked his watch. 'Surely you're due for a break.'

'It doesn't matter. I'd rather be prepared than left floundering when a patient arrives.'

She went to the door, not giving him a chance to object. Luca sighed as she left because what could he have said? That she should stop work and take a break? He wouldn't dream of saying that to any other member of his team and he mustn't single out Kelly for special treatment. If she wanted to work through her break that was her decision. He understood. How many times had he missed a meal—several meals—because he'd been too busy to stop?

He put the file away then settled down at his desk. He phoned his housekeeper first to check that Matteo was all right then pulled out the report he was working on. If Kelly was going to work through her lunch-break, he would too. In a funny way it made him feel less guilty about her working so hard.

He caught himself up short. He had to stop worrying about Kelly and let her get on with her life. Once he started interfering, he might not be able to stop.

CHAPTER THREE

'CIAO.'

Kelly waved goodbye to a couple of nurses who worked on her ward and headed along the path to the staff quarters. It had been a busy day and she was glad it was over. Once she had finished in the clinic, she'd had notes to write up and that had taken the best part of the afternoon. She'd barely finished in time for the afternoon ward round, in fact.

Letizia had made a point of drawing everyone's attention to her when she'd rushed into the ward with just a couple of minutes to spare, but Luca hadn't said a word. In fact, he had ignored her for the next hour and that had been far worse than any reprimand. Even a cutting remark about her tardiness would have been better than the indifference he'd shown her.

She groaned when she realised how stupid she was being. Keying in the security code, she let herself into the building. The air-conditioning was switched on full and she groaned with pleasure when she felt the cool air playing over her skin. The weather had been extremely hot ever since she'd arrived in Sardinia. The temperature regularly hit the mid-thirties and she would have found it very uncomfortable in her apartment without air-conditioning. As she made her way up the stairs, Kelly couldn't help thinking how lucky she was to have been offered an apartment here. From what she could gather, there was a waiting list for staff accommodation, and she had no idea how she'd managed to jump the queue. Unless Luca had arranged it for her?

Her heart lurched at the thought of him going to so much trouble on her behalf before she battened it down. She doubted if he even knew where she lived let alone had played any part in getting her a flat here. She let herself in and went straight to the kitchen and poured herself a glass of mineral water then took it into the sitting room and sat down.

All the apartments were decorated in the same neutral shades of grey and cream. The furniture was standard too, light beech built-in cupboards and cabinets, a small sofa plus an armchair. She'd added a few personal touches—some photos of her and Katie with their parents, a couple of ornaments—but the place still didn't feel like home. It was just somewhere she came to sleep after a busy day. Until she found a place of her own, she would continue to feel like a visitor, although it might be wiser to forget about setting down roots until she decided if she was going to stay.

Kelly sighed when she realised that she was going round in circles. She would have to make up her mind soon about what she intended to do but she was too tired to think about it right now. One of the nurses was celebrating her birthday that night and she had invited Kelly along. They were meeting at a restaurant near the harbour so once she had showered, she changed into white cotton jeans and a black vest top. Her hair always took ages to blow-dry so she scooped it into a ponytail and left it to dry on its own rather than waste time toiling with the hairdryer. Half an hour later she was on her way out again.

She left the hospital and headed towards the harbour, taking the road that overlooked the bay. It was a beautiful evening and the sun was glinting off the azure blue sea. There was a cruise liner anchored in the bay and she could see a flotilla of tenders scurrying back and forth as they ferried the passengers ashore. The air was redolent with the scent of the pine trees which lined one side of the narrow, twisting road. There were a number of luxurious villas built into the hillside, although they were well hidden behind the trees.

It was wonderfully peaceful after living in the centre of busy Manchester and she hated the thought of going back there, but she might have to if she couldn't find a way to work with Luca. Although the day had gone better than she'd feared, she'd felt extremely tense whenever he'd been around and that was hardly conducive to a healthy working relationship. All she could do was wait and see if it got any easier.

Kelly was halfway down the hill when she heard a motorbike roaring along the road behind her. There was a bend coming up so she decided to let the motorbike pass her. A lot of the young men in the area rode motorbikes and they usually rode them at a breakneck speed, so it was safer to keep out of their way.

She'd just stepped onto the grass verge when a movement suddenly caught her eye. A little boy had appeared from the drive of one of the villas and was riding his tricycle down the middle of the road. He was oblivious to the danger he was in and Kelly realised that she would have to do something if she was to avert an accident.

Hurrying forward, she swept the child into her arms just a moment before the motorbike came careering down the road. There was a squeal of brakes as the driver tried to stop, but she didn't wait to see if he succeeded as she hurled herself and the child onto the verge. Pain shot through her when her elbow struck a lump of rock but she barely registered it because she was more concerned about the child. Her legs were trembling as she scrambled to her feet and hurriedly checked him over.

'Good boy,' she said as she ran her hands over his chubby little limbs. Apart from a small graze on his cheek, he appeared unscathed so that was something to be grateful for, although she dreaded to think how the driver had fared.

Picking the child up, she ran over to the young man. He was lying at the side of the road, moaning. Crouching down beside him, Kelly could tell immediately that his right arm was broken. It was an open fracture, too, and she could see a section of bone sticking through the flesh. Setting the little boy on the grass beside her, she took a clean handkerchief out of her bag and placed it over the wound to prevent any infection getting into the tissue. Once that was done, she quickly examined the young man, but he didn't appear to have broken anything else. However, the fact that he wasn't wearing a safety helmet meant that she couldn't rule out the possibility of him having suffered a head injury.

'I'm going to fetch help,' she told him, knowing there was very little else she could do for him. The most important thing now was to get him to hospital as quickly as possible.

He broke into a torrent of rapid Italian and she shook her head. Although her grasp of the language was more than sufficient to deal with the patients she saw at the hospital, he had a thick local accent which made it difficult to follow what he was saying. 'I don't understand.' She pointed towards the villa. 'I'm going for help—*aiuto*.'

Thankfully, he understood what she meant and nodded. Picking up the little boy, Kelly ran back up the road. Hopefully, there would be someone at the villa who would allow her to use their phone to ring for an ambulance.

'Matteo!'

Kelly ground to a halt when a man suddenly appeared from the driveway leading to the villa. She gasped when she recognised Luca because he was the last person she'd expected to see. He came racing towards her and swept the child into his arms.

'What happened?'

'There's been an accident,' she explained as she watched the little boy cling to him. The child obviously knew him, although she had no idea what their relationship was.

'An accident,' Luca repeated, staring at the child in concern.

'Yes, but he's fine. There's just a graze on his cheek—see.' She brushed a dark curl off the little boy's face so that Luca could see what she meant then hurried on. Determining Luca's relationship to the child really wasn't important at the moment. 'This little chap was riding his trike down the road when a motorbike came along. The driver managed to avoid him but he's broken his arm. I was on my way to fetch help when you appeared.'

'I see.' Luca's mouth thinned as he digested what she had told him. Kelly could tell that he was angry and didn't blame him. The child couldn't have been more than two years old, far too young to be out on his own.

'Go up to the house and ask them to phone for an ambulance,' he instructed tersely. 'I'll take a look at the driver while you do that.'

'Right.'

He started to hurry away but Kelly stopped him. 'Do you want me to take the child with me? I expect his mother is wondering where's he's got to.'

Something crossed his face, an expression she found impossible to decipher. 'Thank you but no. I'll keep him here with me.'

He didn't waste time debating the issue as he strode over to the injured motorcyclist. Kelly watched him kneel down beside the man then turned away. She had a feeling that she was missing something but there was no time to worry about it at the moment.

She hurriedly made her way up the drive to the villa. It was a beautiful house, built all on one level, with a small turret at one side and a low-pitched terracotta tiled roof, characteristic of the houses in the area. Crimson bougainvillea spilled down the walls and surrounded the huge oak door with its gleaming brass knocker. At any other time, she would have loved to explore the house and its grounds but it was more important that she sought help for the injured motorcyclist.

She knocked on the door and waited. She could hear footsteps inside and a moment later an elderly woman appeared. *'Si?'*

'I'm sorry to bother you,' Kelly began, 'but there's been an accident outside in the road. Can you phone for an ambulance, please?'

'An accident?' The woman pressed a hand to her mouth. 'Is it Matteo? Has he been hurt?'

'No, no, he's fine,' Kelly assured her. 'It's the driver of the motorcycle who's been injured. Dr Ferrero is with him and he said that you would phone for an ambulance.'

'*Si, si. Immediatamente, signorina.*'

'*Grazie.*' Kelly smiled her thanks then hurried back down the drive. Luca was examining the motorcyclist's left ankle when she went back to them.

'I think he's damaged his ankle as well, possibly sprained it or even torn a ligament,' he told her, glancing up.

'I must have missed that,' she admitted, crouching down beside him. 'I was more concerned about his arm, I'm afraid. Sorry.'

'There is no need to apologise. From what he has told me, the accident could have been a lot more serious if it weren't for you.' He looked over at the little boy, who was happily playing with some pebbles, and she could hear the emotion in his voice when he continued. 'Matteo could have been killed if you hadn't got him out of the way in time, Kelly. I don't know how I can ever thank you.'

'I'm sure the driver would have managed to avoid him,' she said lightly, because she didn't want Luca to think that he was beholden to her in any way.

'Perhaps.'

He didn't say anything else. Maybe he was relieved to have been let off the hook, she thought. She understood if he felt that way because she felt the same. If she was to work with him then she had to maintain her distance—if it was possible to do that, of course.

Fortunately, there was no time to dwell on that thought as the ambulance arrived just then. Luca told the crew what had happened and politely asked Kelly if she wanted to add anything but she shook her head. There was no need, he was too much of a professional to allow anything to get in the way of him doing his job, even his obvious concern for the child.

A frown pleated her brows when she saw the tenderness on his face as he picked up the little boy. Just who was Matteo? And why was he so important to Luca?

Luca could feel his heart thundering as he watched the crew load the injured man into the ambulance. The terror he'd felt when he'd realised that Matteo was missing was impossible to describe. It had felt as though his guts had turned to liquid when he'd seen the open gates and heard the squeal of brakes.

His stomach lurched as he cuddled the child to him, drawing comfort from the feel of his solid little body. Matteo immediately began to squirm in protest at being held so tightly and Luca forced himself to relax his grip. He smiled at him. 'Shall we go home and have a drink?'

'Si, si.'

Matteo clapped his hands in delight. He seemed oblivious to the danger he'd been in and Luca was grateful for that. No child should have to suffer the way he and Sophia had suffered when they'd been children. A child's life should be filled with happiness and love, and certainly not with the terror he had known when he'd been little older than Matteo was now. Cruelty had been a daily part of life at the children's home. There'd been physical beatings and, worse still, mental torture. Being told repeatedly that you were worthless had caused far more damage than the physical abuse had done. Luca knew that he would happily forfeit his life to protect this precious child from that kind of harm.

The thought unlocked a door in his mind usually kept securely locked and he swung round. He wasn't in a fit state to handle the memories at the moment. He had a final word with the paramedics then turned to Kelly, hoping she couldn't tell how emotional he felt. He needed to be in control when he was with her, keep his feelings locked away as securely as those memories of his childhood. It was the only way he was going to cope.

'Would you like to come back to the villa for a cup of coffee?' he offered, hoping she would refuse. Having Kelly in his home would be a mistake. Once she'd been there, he would never be able to rid himself of the memory. He couldn't bear to imagine how hard it would be to sit in the house each night on his own and recall her visit.

'No, thank you,' she said quickly. 'I don't want to be a nuisance.'

'You aren't being a nuisance,' he countered curtly, stung by the speed of her refusal. Did she have to make it quite so obvious that she didn't want anything to do with him?

'I'd still prefer not to come in.' She shrugged, drawing his attention to the fact that the vest top she was wearing had left her shoulders bare apart from two thin little straps.

Luca felt the emotions suddenly gush up inside him again like the bubbles in a champagne bottle once the cork was drawn. He couldn't seem to drag his gaze away from her. Soft evening light was filtering through the trees, painting her milky skin with a golden lustre. She looked like a gilded statue as she stood there, yet he knew that if he touched her it would be flesh and blood he felt, not stone.

His hand half lifted before he realised what he was doing. He couldn't touch her, couldn't smooth his palms over her skin and feel its warmth, and he certainly couldn't dip his head, open his mouth and taste it.

Desire rushed through him, heated his blood, pooled in his loins, and he groaned. He wanted her so badly but it would be wrong to give in to his urges. Even if she felt the same way, it made no difference. He had nothing to offer her now but sex and it wasn't enough, not for him and definitely not for her. Kelly deserved to be loved, wholly and completely and for all eternity. She deserved a man who could give her his heart, his mind and his soul, and he was no longer that man, although he had been once.

'I'm supposed to be meeting some of the staff down at the harbour. It's Catarina's birthday and we're going for a meal. I'd better get off otherwise I'm going to be late.' She lifted her arm to check her watch and Luca frowned when he heard her gasp.

'What's the matter?' he said sharply, because it felt as though he'd been knifed straight through his heart. He could never be the man that Kelly needed and he couldn't begin to describe how wretched that made him feel.

'Nothing. I banged my elbow and it's a bit sore, that's all.'

'Let me see.' Luca put Matteo on the ground and took hold of her arm, frowning when he saw the bruise on her left elbow. 'You need a cold compress on that to reduce the swelling.'

'I'm sure it will be fine,' she said, quickly removing her arm.

'If you want to run the risk of not being able to move your arm for the next week, that's up to you,' he said harshly, even though he knew it wasn't fair to speak to her like that. It wasn't her fault that he felt this way, neither was it her fault that she didn't want to be anywhere near him. After all, he'd been the one who had ended their affair.

The thought set light to his temper and he glowered at her. 'However, I should warn you that I shall take a dim view if you are unable to do your job because you were too stubborn to accept my advice.'

Her face flushed with angry colour. 'Then it appears I don't have a choice, do I?' She shot a derisory glance at the villa. 'I only hope your friends don't mind having a stranger foisted on them so you can play the big tough boss, Luca. It's probably a side of you they haven't seen before. Aren't you afraid it will spoil your image?'

'Not at all. I have never allowed anything to get in the way of doing what I know is right.'

It was nothing less than the truth, but it didn't help him to know that. He could tell that Kelly was furious with him as he led her back to the villa but he didn't care, couldn't allow himself to care. Matteo was chattering away, but for once in his life he was barely listening to what the child was saying. He was too keyed up, too angry, too upset, too…too everything.

'*Papà*.'

Matteo's voice cut through the maelstrom of emotions whirling around inside him and Luca jumped. 'What is it, *caro*?' he asked, ashamed of his selfishness.

He listened carefully while Matteo solemnly told him about the big motorbike that had come down the road and how the lady had picked him up. It was only when he had finished his tale that Luca realised Kelly was standing, stock-still, in the middle of the driveway. There was an expression of shock on her face that scared him when he saw it.

Instinctively, he stepped towards her, but she backed away. Her face was the colour of parchment now that the angry colour had faded and for a moment he wondered if she was going to faint. What if she'd done more than merely bruised her elbow? he thought sickly. What if she'd banged her head and injured herself badly?

'Whose house is this?'Her voice was so low that it sounded as though all the life had seeped out of it, and his fear intensified. Something was seriously wrong and he had no idea what it was.

'I asked you who this villa belongs to,' she repeated in a tone that made him wince.

'Me,' he said simply. 'This is where I live.'

Her eyes closed for a moment before she opened them again and stared at him. 'If this is your house then who is Matteo? Where are his parents?'

Luca felt a wave of sadness wash over him. He knew that his answer was going to hurt her and that there was nothing he could do to prevent it. He had promised Sophia that he would never tell anyone the truth about Matteo's birth and he never had. In the eyes of the law, Matteo was his son and that was what everyone must continue to believe, including Kelly…especially Kelly.

She'd never made any secret of how important her career was to her. She had told him two years ago that she intended to get to the very top and he had believed her. He'd understood her need to succeed because he'd felt the same way. Proving that the people at the home had been wrong to say that he would never amount to anything had spurred him on. It had been a long, hard struggle to reach his present position and he wouldn't have got there if he hadn't remained completely focused.

If Kelly was to achieve her ambitions, she needed to be equally committed. However, if he told her the truth about Matteo then he knew that she would want to help and that was the last thing he could allow to happen. Juggling the demands of parenthood with a career was extremely hard as he knew from experience; some days he wondered how he coped. He certainly wasn't going to put that kind of a burden on her at this stage. The next few years were crucial; she needed to concentrate on learning all she could and couldn't allow anything to distract her. Even though he knew that what he was about to tell her would destroy any good memories she had of their time together, he refused to jeopardise her career.

'Matteo is my son, Kelly. Mine and Sophia's.'

CHAPTER FOUR

'IF YOU'D wait in here, I'll make sure Matteo is all right and come straight back.'

Kelly didn't say a word as she walked into the sitting room—she couldn't. She wasn't even sure how she had got to the villa. She'd just put one foot in front of the other and kept going. Now she could feel herself trembling as she stopped in the middle of the room.

'Sit down and make yourself comfortable. I'll get my housekeeper to bring you a drink. What would you like—tea, coffee, or something cool perhaps?'

'Nothing.' Her voice sounded cracked and thin, like the voice of a very old woman. She cleared her throat because it was important that she maintain her dignity. 'I don't want anything to drink. Thank you.'

'If you're sure...?'

Luca let the question trail off but she didn't answer him. She'd used up every scrap of strength and had nothing more to give. She sat down on the sofa after he left the room and closed her eyes. She could feel her heart beating, hear herself breathing and knew she was alive. It was just the core of her that had died, the vital spark that made her who she was. It had been snuffed out by those words: Matteo is my son. Mine and Sophia's.

Pain welled up inside her and she bit her lip. The only positive thought she'd had to cling to these past two years was that there'd been nothing premeditated about the way Luca had treated her. Now she could see what a fool she'd been to believe that. Luca had carried on an affair with her even though he must have known that Sophia was pregnant.

Tears swam to her eyes but she blinked them away. By the time Luca reappeared, she had herself under control. She obeyed without question when he placed a small table in front of the sofa and told her to rest her arm on it. He'd brought a basin of water and a towel with him, and she didn't object when he bathed her elbow. She didn't care if he touched her. She was numb, immune to him now, inured against any future pain by his past betrayal.

'This should help to reduce the swelling.' He wrung out the towel and wrapped it around her elbow. 'You'll still have a bruise in the morning but this should alleviate some of the stiffness at least.'

'Thank you.' Kelly barely glanced at him as she stood up. 'I'll let you have the towel back tomorrow.'

'Don't worry about it,' he said dismissively.

'I would prefer to return it,' she said, walking to the door. She crossed the marble-floored hallway without glancing either to left or right. Any desire she'd had to explore the house had disappeared. She was no longer interested in it or its owner.

She stopped when she reached the front door and turned to look at him. Ever since she'd discovered they would be working together, she had been afraid that she wouldn't be able to separate Luca, the man she had loved, from Luca, her boss, but it was no longer a problem. The person standing before her was a stranger, someone who had lied and cheated to get what he'd wanted. She couldn't even feel angry about what he had done; she just felt numb.

'Are you sure you feel all right? You don't have a headache, do you?'

'I'm fine,' she said flatly. 'I'll see you in the morning.'

'Of course.'

He didn't say anything else as he let her out. Kelly didn't look back as she made her way down the drive. She had no idea if he was watching her, but it didn't matter if he was. He meant nothing to her now. He was just someone she worked with, someone she could learn from so she could improve her skills. The children she treated would benefit from her knowing Luca, but for her, personally, it was a matter of indifference.

It was only when she reached the end of the drive and discovered that she couldn't see where she was going that she realised she was crying. Tears were pouring down her face, blinding her so that she stumbled and had to grab hold of the gate to steady herself. Luca had had a child with another woman. Sophia had been carrying his baby while he'd been making love to her. What kind of a man slept with another woman when his girlfriend was pregnant?

'Kelly? Are you all right? What's happened?'

All of a sudden Luca was there and she rounded on him in fury. 'How could you, Luca? How could you sleep with me when Sophia was expecting your child?'

'Because I had no idea she was pregnant!' He caught hold of her arms and held onto them when she tried to pull away. 'I only found out about the baby when I returned to Italy.'

'You really expect me to believe that?' she scoffed.

'Yes, because it's the truth.' His grey eyes flashed as he gripped her even harder and she winced as his fingers bit into her bruised arm. He uttered something harsh as he swiftly released her. 'I'm sorry. I didn't mean to hurt you, Kelly.'

'Didn't you?' she said brokenly.

'No.' He ran a gentle finger down her cheek and wiped away a tear. 'Not now and most definitely not then. You were far too precious to me.'

'Don't,' she pleaded, because she couldn't bear to hear him say such things when they weren't true. 'Please, don't say anything else, Luca. I don't want to hear it.'

'I know and I don't blame you, either. But you have to believe that I never meant any of this to happen. All I've ever wanted was to protect you, Kelly.' He cupped her cheek with his hand and his eyes were filled with sadness. 'I know I failed in the past, but I swear that I won't fail again.'

She wasn't sure what he meant and didn't care. She twisted her head to the side so that he was forced to release her. 'I don't want you to protect me. I suggest you concentrate on your wife and your son from now on and leave me alone.' She laughed harshly, whipping up her anger rather than give in to the despair that threatened to overwhelm her. 'I wonder what Sophia would say if she found out that you were making promises like that to another woman. Or maybe it's something you do on a regular basis and she's used to it? Perhaps I should ask her.'

'That isn't possible,' he said roughly.

'No?' She shrugged. 'I can understand you not wanting us to meet but don't worry, Luca. I'll be very discreet. I won't say a word about the fact that you were sleeping with me when she was pregnant.'

'Sophia is dead.'

The words cut through the still evening air and Kelly gasped. She stared at him in horror. 'Dead?'

'Yes. She died eighteen months ago.'

'But Matteo must have been only a baby,' she said blankly.

'He was six months old.' Luca took a deep breath, but the pain in his voice was so raw that it brought fresh tears to her eyes. 'She had a highly aggressive form of breast cancer.'

'And there was nothing anyone could do for her?' she whispered.

'If she'd received treatment as soon as it was diagnosed then she might have had a chance, but the odds were always stacked against her.'

'What do you mean, *if* she'd received treatment sooner? What was to stop her having it immediately?'

'Sophia found out that she had cancer the same week she discovered she was pregnant.' He ran his hand over his face and Kelly could tell how much it hurt him to talk about what had happened. 'She refused to undergo any treatment in case it harmed the baby. Her consultant pleaded with her, but she refused. In her eyes, it would have been tantamount to killing her child.'

'And did you know about this?' Kelly asked, appalled. 'Did she tell you that she had refused treatment?'

'No. I had no idea that Sophia was pregnant let alone that she had cancer until I returned to Italy. She was eight months pregnant by then and I managed to persuade her to have a Caesarean so she could begin chemotherapy. However, we both knew it was unlikely to help very much. In the event, it gave her a couple more months to spend with Matteo.'

'I don't know what to say… It must have been awful…for both of you.' She tailed off and he sighed.

'It was much, much worse for Sophia. She knew that she wasn't going to live to see her son grow up and that's what scared her more than anything else. Once she was sure that Matteo would be cared for, she accepted what was happening. She was extremely brave right until the end. It was humbling to watch the way she coped with her illness.'

'Is that why you got married so soon after you returned to Italy?' Kelly said quietly. One of the things that had hurt her most had been the speed with which Luca had married, but now she understood why it had happened so quickly. He must have been desperate to save Sophia from any more heartache.

Her heart lifted as she realised that it cast a different light on the events of the past. However, it would be wrong to get too carried away. She must never forget that it had been Sophia he'd loved, not her.

'*Si.* There was no point waiting when it was the one thing that would set Sophia's mind at rest.' He stared at the ground for a moment and when he looked up, she could see the plea in his eyes. 'I meant what I said, Kelly. I never intended to hurt you. I just didn't have a choice.'

'So, Alessandro, how do you feel today?' Luca stopped beside the boy's bed. It was the start of the morning ward round and Alessandro Alessi was the first patient on his list. He reviewed Alessandro's notes while the boy explained that he was feeling much better that day.

The CT scan had shown no sign of an obstruction and Luca had concluded that the excess of cerebrospinal fluid had been caused by a fresh bout of infection. He'd prescribed another course of antibiotics and they appeared to be working, although he had no intention of rushing things. Alessandro was due to be discharged the following day, but he decided that he would keep him in hospital while they monitored the situation. There was no point taking any chances at this stage.

'I'm glad you're feeling better,' he told the boy with a smile. 'However, I think it would be wise if you stayed in the hospital for a few more days. Hopefully, you'll be well enough to go home after the weekend.'

Alessandro's face fell. 'But it's my birthday on Friday. I was going to have a party and all my friends were coming.'

'I'm very sorry,' Luca said sympathetically, knowing how important birthdays were to children. 'Maybe you can have your party another day?'

'It won't be the same,' Alessandro muttered, closing his eyes and refusing to look at him.

Luca sighed. He didn't enjoy being the bearer of bad news but the child's health was more important than being considered the villain of the piece. He moved away from the bed, feeling the weight of that thought pressing down on him. All night long he had struggled with his conscience. Part of him knew that he should have told Kelly the truth about Sophia and Matteo while he'd had the chance, but another part was afraid of the harm it might have caused.

He knew what Kelly was like, knew that her tender heart would be touched by the story, but he didn't want her getting involved in his affairs when it could have a detrimental effect on her career. Even in these enlightened times, it was harder for a woman to reach the top than it was for a man. Although lip service was paid to the idea of equality between the sexes, he had seen many times how a woman candidate for a job would be passed over because she had a family. Was he really prepared to let that happen to Kelly? Of course not.

Luca's mouth set as he led the group to the next bed. Letizia was standing next to him and he turned to her. Kelly was standing behind him and he needed to be sure that he was in control of his emotions before he spoke to her.

'Have the lab results for this patient come back yet, Dr Sentini?'

'I shall check and see.' Letizia gave him a seductive smile as she picked up the notes. '*Si*. Here they are. The patient's white cell count is elevated—just as you suspected, *dottore*.'

Luca ignored the fawning note in her voice. If Letizia hoped to gain extra points by toadying to him, she would be disappointed. He took the report from her and glanced through the figures then handed it to Carlo, the senior registrar. In a normal blood sample there should be approximately seven and a half thousand white blood cells per cubic millimetre of blood. Six-year-old Ilaria's results showed a massive increase in this number and that the cells were abnormal in shape and immature as well. There were also far fewer red cells and platelets than there should have been.

'Can you outline the symptoms the child presented with when she was admitted,' Luca instructed, glancing at Letizia again.

'Fever, enlargement of the lymphatic glands and spleen,' Letizia recited, reading from the notes. 'Her parents also reported that she'd had a rash, although there was no sign of it when she was admitted.' She shrugged. 'All classic symptoms of some kind of viral infection.'

'And what would you conclude, having seen the results of the blood tests?' he asked her.

'That it's obviously a viral infection,' Letizia declared.

'So you wouldn't request any further tests?'

She shook her head. 'No. I would wait for the child's immune system to fight the effects of the illness. The few anti-viral drugs that are available can cause severe side effects.'

'That's very true,' he agreed. 'However, I doubt if sitting back and waiting will be effective in this instance.' Letizia's smile faded abruptly when he turned to Kelly. 'What would you do, Dr Carlyon?'

'I'd order a bone-marrow biopsy.'

'To check for what exactly?' he shot back.

'An abnormal number of blast cells.' She shrugged, although he could tell that she wasn't as relaxed as she was pretending to be. Had she spent the night thinking about what he had told her? He knew it was so and despite his resolve not to involve her in his affairs, he found himself drawing comfort from the thought.

'And if there are blast cells present?' He chased away that foolish notion because he couldn't afford to weaken. 'What might that indicate?'

'That it could be an acute form of leukaemia.' She looked him straight in the eyes, letting him know that if this was a test then she was equal to the challenge. 'I would also request a lumbar puncture so the cerebrospinal fluid could be checked for blast cells as well.'

'I see.' He turned to Carlo. 'What do you think, Dr Baldovini? Do you agree with your colleague that we should follow that route?'

'*Si.*' Carlo smiled warmly at Kelly. 'I think Dr Carlyon is quite right to suggest both procedures. It is what I would recommend.'

'It appears we are in full agreement, then.'

Luca turned away because he didn't trust himself not to say something he would regret. It had nothing to do with him if Carlo found Kelly attractive. He sent the team to the next patient while he filled in the necessary forms for the lab. Fortunately, Ilaria's parents had remained in the hospital with her so he was able to get their consent for the test to go ahead.

Little Ilaria started crying when he gently explained that he needed to take a sample of fluid from her spine, and that made him feel worse than ever. As he waited while the child's mother tried to calm her down, he found himself wishing that he had asked Kelly to stay behind and help. She was wonderful with children and had a real gift when it came to soothing their fears.

He caught himself up short. Kelly had her job to do and he had his. He was supposed to be helping her, not the other way round. He must concentrate on passing on his knowledge to her, and that would be more than enough compensation for what he was going to miss personally.

He groaned under his breath because nothing would make up for losing her and there was no point pretending that it would. He had to face up to how he felt and deal with his feelings if he was to treat Kelly as just another colleague. And if that meant stepping aside while Carlo or anyone else made advances to her, that's what he had to do. After all, it was up to Kelly whom she dated.

It sounded very sensible in theory, but as Luca rubbed a little anaesthetic into the child's spine before he drew off the fluid, he knew how difficult it was going to be to put it into practice. The thought of watching Kelly with another man was more than he could bear when he wanted her himself.

CHAPTER FIVE

THEY were in Luca's office, reviewing the morning's case notes, when the telephone rang. Luca had stayed behind to speak to Ilaria's parents after the ward round had finished so Carlo was chairing the meeting. Kelly was nearest to the phone so she picked up the receiver. It was a nurse from Pronto Soccorso—the emergency department—with a message for Luca, asking him to contact the consultant on duty as soon as possible.

Kelly excused herself and went to find him. He'd mentioned something about taking Ilaria's parents to one of the family suites so she made her way there. There were three self-contained units available for the use of any families that wished to stay in the hospital. Each suite comprised a bedroom with a double bed and twin bunk beds, a bathroom, and a sitting room with a microwave oven and a kettle. She checked which suite Ilaria's parents were using and knocked on the door, but they told her that Luca had already left.

She frowned as she backtracked along the corridor. It was unusual for him to disappear like this. Normally, he was punctilious about letting them know where he was in case they needed him. She decided to try the ward in case he'd gone back there, but once again she drew a blank. She was about to go back to his office and ask the switchboard to page him when she spotted him getting out of the lift.

'Luca, wait,' she called, hurrying after him.

'Yes?' He stopped, his face betraying very little as he turned to her. 'Did you want me?'

'Yes. Pronto Soccorso just phoned,' Kelly explained, careful to keep any hint of emotion out of her voice. She'd spent the night thinking about what he had told her about Sophia. Despite the heartache she'd suffered when he'd left her, she would never have wished for that to happen. She knew that if he'd given the smallest hint that she could help him in any way she wouldn't have hesitated, but he'd made it clear that he didn't expect anything from her.

She hurried on, not wanting to dwell on that thought when it was so painful. 'They want you to get in touch with the consultant on duty as soon as possible. It sounded urgent.'

'*Grazie.*'

Luca immediately veered off and went to the nursing station. Picking up the phone, he dialled Pronto Soccorso. Kelly hesitated, unsure whether she should stay until he'd finished or return to the meeting. Carlo sometimes took a slightly different approach than Luca did when it came to dealing with their patients and it might help her gain a different perspective on a couple of the cases she'd seen that morning.

'*Si, si. Immediatamente. Bene.*'

Kelly was about to slip away when she heard Luca drop the receiver onto its rest. 'Problems?'

'There's a child been taken ill on a cruise ship that's anchored in the bay. Apparently, the ship's doctor is on shore leave and the nurse is unable to contact him. She's requested our help so I'm going to go out there and see what's happened.'

'Why did Pronto Soccorso ask you to go?' Kelly asked curiously as she followed him to the lift.

'They have a number of staff off sick at the moment,' he explained, pressing the button. 'Add to that the fact that one of the school buses crashed this morning, injuring several dozen children, although mostly just cuts and bruises, and you can understand why they need all the help they can get.'

'I certainly can!' Kelly exclaimed. She stepped back when the lift arrived. 'I'll let everyone know where you're going, shall I?'

'If you wouldn't mind,' he began, then paused. 'You're not rostered for clinic this morning, are you?'

Kelly shook her head. 'No, it's Letizia this morning. Oh, and Selina is helping Carlo, I believe,' she added, suddenly remembering that Carlo had asked the junior house officer if she would like to sit in.

'In that case, I'd like you to come with me.' Luca held the lift door open when it started to close. 'I might need a hand and it will be good experience for you to deal with a situation beyond what you might expect to encounter within the hospital.'

'Are you sure you want to take me with you?' Kelly said uncertainly. She shrugged when he raised his brows. 'I don't mind covering for Letizia if you'd prefer to take her.'

'If I'd wanted Letizia to accompany me, I would have asked her,' he said shortly.

Kelly flushed as she realised that she was in danger of making a fool of herself. This wasn't a social outing but a professional visit, and as far as Luca was concerned that was all that mattered.

'Of course,' she murmured as she hurriedly stepped into the lift.

They made their way to the ground floor. Luca stopped at the reception desk and asked the receptionist to send a message to Carlo to tell him that he and Kelly would be unavailable for the next couple of hours. Carlo should contact Pronto Soccorso if he needed any further details as to their whereabouts.

Kelly bit her lip as she followed him to the supplies office, where he signed for a medical kit. Maybe Luca felt that it was explanation enough for their absence, but there would be a lot of speculation about them disappearing together, and it was the last thing she wanted. She wanted everyone to believe that she and Luca had a strictly professional relationship. That was why she hadn't told anyone that she had met him when he'd been working in England. She knew how quickly gossip could spread and now, more than ever, she didn't want to find herself at the centre of a scandal. Even though it could no longer hurt Sophia if the story got out, Kelly hated the thought of people finding out that she and Luca had been having an affair while his wife had been pregnant.

She sighed because it wasn't just her reputation she was worried about. She had believed Luca when he'd told her that he hadn't known about the baby, but would others believe that, too? People were so quick to judge and she hated the thought of him losing the respect of his colleagues. It would be so unfair if he had to cope with that kind of upset after everything else he had suffered.

Kelly took a deep breath as she followed him out of the

main doors, her mind made up. Nobody would ever find out about their affair from her.

Luca pulled into a parking space and switched off the engine. Kelly had been unusually quiet on the drive to the harbour. Was she worried about being alone with him after last night? he wondered. Maybe she thought that he'd been clearing the way so he could hit on her again but that couldn't be further from the truth. Now, more than ever, he needed to keep her at a distance.

He sighed as he opened the car door. He'd found it extremely stressful to be around her that morning. That was why he'd gone to the canteen after he'd spoken to Ilaria's parents. He'd needed some time on his own and it had helped to a point, but the veneer of calm was wafer thin.

It would take very little to tip him over the edge and he couldn't let that happen. He had to stick to his decision and treat Kelly as just another member of his team. Maybe he had asked her to accompany him on this visit but it was purely because she was the logical choice. He hefted the case of medical supplies out of the boot, ignoring the insidious little voice in his head that was insisting he could have asked someone else if he'd wanted to. He'd asked Kelly and that was the end of it.

'The tenders tie up over there,' he explained, pointing across the harbour to where a procession of small boats were ferrying the passengers to and from the ship.

'I've never seen a ship that size before,' Kelly admitted as she stared across the bay to where the cruise ship was lying at anchor.

'They seem to get bigger every year,' Luca agreed, leading

the way along the quay. He sidestepped a group of passengers who were making their way ashore then picked up his pace, wanting to get on board the ship as quickly as possible.

'I wonder how many passengers the ship carries,' Kelly mused as she strode along beside him. She had no difficulty keeping up with him, her long legs easily matching his brisk pace. Tall and slender with an athletic figure and that glorious red hair, she seemed oblivious to the admiring glances she attracted from the people they passed.

Luca felt a little flurry of something in the pit of his stomach and stamped down hard on it. He wouldn't allow himself to feel jealous. He'd already decided that he had no right to interfere in her life and he would stick to it, come what may. He carefully erased any trace of emotion from his voice as he replied.

'A liner that size probably carries close to two thousand passengers plus half that number again of crew.'

'Really?' Her eyes widened as she stared at the ship in amazement. 'That's three thousand people. It's almost the size of a small town.'

Luca laughed, enjoying her reaction despite his determination not to get involved. 'It's probably bigger than a lot of the towns around here.'

Kelly shook her head. 'I can't imagine the logistics of feeding that many people, can you?'

'It's not just feeding them,' he pointed out, leading the way to one of the tenders. 'You also have to keep them entertained and make sure they stay safe and healthy as well.'

'No wonder they have their own medical team on board.'

'It's absolutely essential,' Luca concurred.

They had reached the security checkpoint now and their

way was barred by a member of the ship's crew. He explained who they were and showed the officer his hospital identity badge. Kelly did the same and then they were both asked to wait while their photographs were taken. A few minutes later they were issued with passes that allowed them access to the ship.

Kelly frowned as she attached her pass to her blouse. 'I didn't realise that security would be so tight.'

'The operators of the cruise liners have stepped up security because of the risk of terrorism,' he explained, leading the way to the tender.

'Really?' She shuddered. 'It's awful to think that someone might deliberately set out to harm the passengers, isn't it?'

'It's a sign of the times, unfortunately.' He showed his pass to the crew then stepped on board, turning to give Kelly a hand.

'Thanks.'

She gave him a quick smile then went and sat down near the bow of the vessel. However, it was a moment before he followed her. It was just a smile, he told himself sternly as he took his place beside her on the hard plastic seat. It hadn't meant anything and certainly nothing to have caused this riot of emotions churning inside him.

He made himself comfortable and stared straight ahead. He had to forget about everything else and concentrate on what they would find when they reached the ship. The details he'd been given were very sketchy. All he knew was that the patient was an eight-year-old girl who had presented with pain in the back and blood-stained urine. Her temperature was slightly elevated although there was no sign of fever.

The boat suddenly lurched as it left the calmer waters of

the harbour and sailed out into the bay, and Luca lost his concentration. Before he could stop himself, his gaze slid sideways and he felt his heart contract when he found himself staring at Kelly's profile. She was so beautiful that any man would want her, but it wasn't just her looks that had attracted him when they'd met—it had been everything about her. She was intelligent and kind, compassionate and thoughtful, too. She genuinely cared about the children she treated and wanted to do everything she could for them.

Her dedication had always appealed to him as much as her looks; he had loved her spirit as well as her body. He knew that if he was asked to describe his perfect woman, he would have described Kelly—kind, beautiful, loving, dedicated Kelly.

She was everything he had ever wanted, but he couldn't have her. He couldn't risk destroying a part of her he loved so much. Her career was as important to him as it was to her because it helped to define who she was.

Emotion tightened his guts as the futility of his feelings hit him afresh but he couldn't afford to indulge himself. Kelly was extremely astute and she would soon realise how he felt about her if he wasn't careful. She might hate him now for what he had done to her in the past, but he sensed that her hatred could change very easily to love. He could see it in her eyes whenever she looked at him. Part of her wanted to hate him, but underneath all the anger and the pain love still existed.

He knew it would take very little to make Kelly love him again and although it was tempting, he couldn't do it. He had to drive her away so she could fulfil her dreams, but every time he pushed her away, he would be destroying part of himself.

CHAPTER SIX

'I DIDN'T know what to do for the best. Dr Ashworth is supposed to take his pager with him when he goes ashore, but he hasn't responded to my calls.'

The ship's nurse sounded worried as she led them along the passageway and Kelly hastened to reassure her. 'You did exactly the right thing by contacting the hospital.'

'Do you think so?' The woman sighed as she stopped outside one of the cabins. 'I just hope I don't get a rollicking for calling you in. It's my first trip, and I hope it doesn't turn out to be my last.'

'As Dr Carlyon said, you did the right thing,' Luca said firmly. 'It is better to err on the side of caution when dealing with a young child.'

'That's what I thought.' The nurse visibly brightened. She smiled warmly at Luca as she knocked on the cabin door. 'Thanks. You've really cheered me up.'

Kelly didn't say anything. Obviously, Luca's opinion carried far more weight than hers had done, she thought irritably. She gave herself a mental shake when she realised that her annoyance stemmed more from jealousy than professional pique. Luca was an extremely handsome man, after all, and she couldn't blame the nurse for being dazzled by him.

The child's mother opened the cabin door and quickly ushered them inside. 'I'm so glad you're here. I've been worried sick. Chloe was fine yesterday but she's been complaining that her back and her tummy hurt ever since she woke up this morning.'

'I believe you noticed there was blood in her urine?' Luca said as he made his way to the bed.

'That's right. It wasn't a lot but it really frightened me when I saw it,' the mother admitted. 'That's why I called the medical centre and asked to see the doctor.'

'You did the right thing,' Luca repeated, using the same tone he'd used with the nurse.

Kelly knew it was silly but she couldn't help feeling pleased that he hadn't been singling out the nurse for special treatment. She hurriedly pushed that unworthy thought to the back of her mind as she took out a pad and a pen to write up the case history while Luca set about examining the little girl.

'My name is Dr Ferrero,' he told the child. 'I work in a special hospital for children and Dr Carlyon works with me. I'm going to feel your tummy first, Chloe, and ask you some questions, if that's OK with you?'

The child nodded shyly. With her mass of blonde curls and huge blue eyes, she looked like a little angel as she lay passively in the bed while Luca gently palpated her abdomen.

'That's a very good girl,' he praised her. He glanced over his shoulder at Kelly. 'No sign of abdominal tension or obvious tenderness.'

Kelly nodded as she jotted down his findings on the pad.

She knew that he was ruling out the most likely cause of the child's illness first—appendicitis. That usually started with tenderness around the navel which gradually developed into a more localised pain in the lower right-hand side of the abdomen. Sometimes the appendix could impinge on the ureter and cause blood-stained urine, too.

'Has Chloe had a viral infection recently?' he asked the child's mother.

'I don't think so,' Mrs Robinson replied uncertainly. She looked round when the cabin door opened and sighed in relief when she saw the man who had entered the cabin. 'Chloe hasn't had a viral infection, has she, John?' she said, addressing her question to the newcomer.

'She had a bit of a sore throat about a week ago,' he explained as he came over to the bed. 'It only lasted a couple of days and she's been fine since then. I really can't see that it's caused all this.'

'I wish you'd told me!' his wife exclaimed, and he grimaced.

'Sorry. I just never thought to mention it.'

'I'm Luca Ferrero, head of clinical care at Santa Margherita's hospital.' Luca held out his hand. It was obvious that he wanted to keep the conversation on track and not allow a row to develop between the parents. He turned and politely included Kelly in his introductions. 'This is my colleague, Dr Carlyon.'

'Good to meet you both,' the man replied, shaking Kelly's hand as well. 'I'm John Robinson, Chloe's father.' He glanced at his wife and sighed. 'Sorry. We're a bit on edge at the moment, you understand. Wendy has been working away so I've been looking after Chloe and her brother, Daniel. That's why Wendy didn't know about Chloe's throat infection.'

'And your son hasn't complained of feeling ill as well?'
Luca queried.

'No, he's fine. I've just taken him to the kids' club and left
him there, causing havoc.'

Everyone laughed and Kelly was relieved when Mrs
Robinson joined in. The last thing they needed was for the
parents to start arguing. Luca turned to her and lowered his
voice. 'It could be mesenteric lymphadenitis. We'll order a
blood test to check for any signs of infection.'

Kelly nodded as she made a note on her pad. Mesenteric
lymphadenitis occurred when the lymph nodes in the peri-
toneum became inflamed following a viral infection. The
symptoms mimicked those of appendicitis, making it extremely difficult to diagnose correctly. She waited while Luca
continued his examination, enjoying watching him work. He
was quick but thorough, leaving nothing to chance as he continued to gently question the child. He nodded when the little
girl shyly explained that her back hurt more than her tummy.

'And is it a big sharp pain or more of an ache?'

Chloe thought about that. 'It's like when I had toothache
but it's in my back this time.'

'I see. That was a really good way to describe it. Well
done.'

The little girl smiled, delighted by the praise. Luca carefully rolled her over onto her side and felt her kidneys,
stopping when she whimpered. 'It looks as though that's
where it hurts the most,' he said, gently rolling her onto her
back again.

Kelly frowned when she saw him bend over the child and
examine her eyes, testing the flesh beneath her lower lids with
his fingertip. He looked up and she could see real concern in

his eyes. 'There's definite signs of puffiness around her eyes. I'd like a urine test done if you could sort it out, please, Kelly.'

'Of course,' Kelly murmured. She found a sample jar in the medical pack and handed it to Chloe's mother. 'Can you help Chloe provide us with a urine specimen? We have a test kit with us so we can check it while we're here to save time.'

'Of course.' Mrs Robinson helped her daughter out of the bed. Kelly could tell how worried she was but she put on a brave face for her daughter's sake. 'Come along, poppet. The doctor needs you to pee into this tiny little pot! Let's see if you manage it.'

Chloe giggled as her mother and the nurse helped her to the bathroom. Mr Robinson went with them and waited outside the door. Kelly turned to Luca as soon as the family were out of earshot. 'What do you think it is?'

'It's still very much guesswork at this stage, but I'm thinking along the lines of glomerulonephritis.' He shrugged. 'It's often triggered by a bacterial infection—something like strep throat, for instance. The patient's immune system makes antibodies to fight off the infection. Sometimes they combine with the bacterial antigens and form particles that circulate in the bloodstream and become trapped in the glomeruli.'

'And that causes inflammation in the kidneys' filtering units which damages them and stops them working properly,' she finished for him.

'Exactly. Once that happens, the damaged glomeruli allow red blood cells to pass straight into the urine and that's why you get the staining. Protein also escapes into the urine and causes oedema.'

'Which is why you were so concerned when you realised that Chloe's eyes were puffy!' she exclaimed.

'Yes. Puffiness around the eyes is one of the symptoms I would expect to find in a case like that.'

'I would never, ever have reached that conclusion so quickly,' Kelly admitted. She stared at him in admiration. 'You are just brilliant, Luca. I wish I was half the physician you are.'

Luc felt his heart swell with pride when he heard the warmth in her voice. Even though he knew that he needed to keep a rein on his feelings, he couldn't help being touched by her praise. He cleared his throat, trying to batten down the happiness which filled him.

'Carry on the way you're doing and you will soon outstrip me. You have it within your power to be the very best there is, Kelly, so long as you don't allow yourself to be sidetracked.'

'There's not much likelihood of that happening,' she said flatly, all the warmth suddenly disappearing from her voice. 'You know the old saying, once bitten, twice shy? Well, I've adopted it as my motto. I'm only interested in my job now, nothing else.'

Luca's heart ached when he realised that he was responsible for her present attitude. He hated himself for hurting her, even though he'd had no choice. It was a relief when the Robinsons returned because it meant he could put that thought out of his mind for the moment at least.

Kelly opened the packet of dipsticks and set about testing the urine sample. It didn't take long to get the results and he nodded when he saw that they confirmed his suspicions. There was an excess of protein in Chloe's urine which indicated the child could be suffering from glomerulonephritis.

Chloe would need to be admitted to hospital while more tests were carried out to confirm his diagnosis. She would also need to undergo a kidney-function test to measure how well her kidneys were working. Severe hypertension was a serious side effect of glomerulonephritis and they couldn't afford for there to be any delay in moving her to the hospital. It would mean the family having to cut short their holiday.

Luca led the parents away from the bed while he broke the news to them. 'I'm going to admit Chloe to hospital. I'm afraid it's the only option in the circumstances.'

'Hospital,' Mrs Robinson gasped, clutching hold of her husband's hand. 'But can't you just give her something to clear up the infection if that's what has caused all this?'

'I'm afraid it's not that simple. It looks as though Chloe has something called glomerulonephritis and it is potentially extremely serious.'

'Glomeru—what on earth is that, Doctor?' John Robinson demanded.

'To explain it in simple terms, the glomeruli, or filtering units, in Chloe's kidneys have become inflamed and her kidneys are no longer working properly. She needs to go to hospital so we can determine how severe the situation is. The urine test confirmed that there is protein in her urine and that's causing oedema—swelling.'

He waited a moment to make sure they had understood then carried on, trying not to listen to Kelly's voice in the background as she spoke to the child, but it was impossible to blank it out completely. Something warm and alive began to trickle through him, a feeling he hadn't experienced in a long time. It was sheer pleasure he could feel, and he didn't deserve it, couldn't afford to feel it when it could put Kelly's future at risk.

'It's an indication that Chloe's kidney function is already impaired so we cannot afford to delay any longer. She needs to be in hospital so that she can be treated with antibiotics to clear up the infection. She will also need support if her kidneys stop functioning.'

'And that could happen?' John Robinson said hoarsely as the true severity of the situation hit him.

'It's a risk, yes. However, we will do everything in our power to avoid that eventuality.'

'Then we don't have a choice, do we, Wendy?' Mr Robinson put his arm around his wife as she started to cry. 'Come on now, love, pull yourself together. What's a holiday compared to our Chloe being really poorly?'

'You're right.' Wendy blew her nose. 'You go and fetch Daniel while I throw some clothes into a bag. The ship won't wait and we don't know how long we're going to be here so we'd better take some stuff with us.'

'You'll be able to stay at the hospital,' Luca explained, pleased to see how well they were responding to the crisis. 'There's accommodation available for family use and one of the units will be free this afternoon. You're welcome to use it.'

'Thank you. You've been really kind, Doctor,' Wendy said sincerely. Luca turned to the ship's nurse as Mrs Robinson went away to start packing. 'Can you inform the captain about what's happened? I'll arrange for an ambulance to pick us up at the harbour, but we'll need a stretcher to get Chloe onto the tender so can you organise that as well?'

'I can't believe this.' The young woman groaned. 'It's just my luck that something like this has to happen when Dr Ashworth has gone AWOL.'

'I'm sure you'll manage,' he said briskly, because he didn't have the time to listen to her complaints. He went back to Kelly. 'I'm going to arrange for an ambulance to meet us at the harbour.'

'Fine. I'll get everything ready so we can be on our way as soon as it arrives.'

'Thanks.'

He gave her a quick and, hopefully, cool smile then stepped out onto the balcony and used his mobile phone to call the hospital. Once the ambulance was sorted out, he contacted the switchboard and asked them to page Carlo. His senior registrar came on the line a few moments later and listened intently as Luca explained what had happened and what needed to be done in readiness for their arrival. The renal unit would have to be alerted too, but Carlo promised to have everything ready for them.

When he went back into the cabin, the Robinsons were ready to leave. Luca glanced at his watch, hoping it wouldn't take the crew too long to fetch that stretcher. Every extra minute put Chloe in even greater danger. It was a relief when there was a knock on the door and two officers arrived with the stretcher.

The embarkation point for the tenders was on A deck so they took the little girl down in one of the lifts. There was a queue of passengers waiting to go ashore but they were ushered straight through. Two of the crew from the tender helped them transfer the stretcher on board. Mr and Mrs Robinson and their son were next to board followed by him and Kelly.

Luca stepped onto the tender then offered her his hand, feeling his pulse leap when he felt her fingers grip his as she stepped across the gap between the ship and the boat. The small craft bobbed up and down as it took their weight and she clung to him for a second until it had stopped rocking.

'Thanks. I think I've got my sea legs now,' she quipped, letting go of his hand.

She made her way straight to where the crew had deposited the stretcher and crouched down to speak to Chloe, but Luca's heart continued to bob up and down like a cork on water. He closed his eyes as despair gripped him. He could tell himself a million times that he had no business feeling this way but it made no difference. His body ached for her, his heart yearned for her, and his mind wouldn't accept that he couldn't have her. Every bit of him seemed to be focused on one crazy, wonderful thought and that was getting Kelly back.

Just for a second he let his mind run riot. If he had her back in his life, he would be the happiest man alive. He would have Matteo and the woman he loved, and he wouldn't want anything else. Even his career didn't matter to him as much as Kelly did. There was nothing he wouldn't do to have her, keep her, love her, live with her for the rest of his life—nothing except sacrifice her career.

Pain lanced through him as he opened his eyes because everything came back to that. No matter how much he longed for her, he couldn't take away the things she held most dear.

CHAPTER SEVEN

THE journey back to the hospital was uneventful. Within a very short time, Chloe had been settled into the ward. Kelly checked the child's obs then went to the office to write up her case notes. Although she could have left it until after lunch, she preferred to get the job done immediately in case Luca needed to refer to them. She sighed as she sat down. If she was hoping to earn herself a few extra brownie points, she was undoubtedly wasting her time. Luca wouldn't be impressed by her dedication. He wasn't impressed by anything she did.

It was a depressing thought and she tried not to dwell on it as she carefully copied out the notes she'd made. She read through what she'd written then signed her name at the bottom once she was sure that she'd missed nothing out. All she had to do now was file them away and she could go for lunch.

She went to the filing cabinet then glanced round when the door opened and felt her heart sink when she saw Letizia come into the office. She and Letizia hadn't hit if off from the moment they had met. Whilst the rest of the team had made her feel very welcome, Letizia had treated her with barely concealed animosity from the outset. Kelly wasn't sure what the problem was, although she suspected it had something to do with Luca. However, if Letizia imagined that Luca was interested in her, she was mistaken. He had made it abundantly clear last night that he wanted nothing to do with her outside working hours.

'I was just writing up Chloe Robinson's case history,' Kelly explained, making a determined effort to get along with the other woman. She didn't want there to be any bad feeling between her and Letizia when they had to work together. 'The little girl we brought in off the ship.'

'How clever of you to persuade Luca to take you with him,' Letizia retorted. 'I'm sure it helped to get you into his good books.'

'I didn't persuade him,' Kelly denied. 'He asked me to accompany him and I went. I had absolutely no say in the matter.'

'Whatever.' Letizia shrugged, making it clear that she didn't believe her. She ignored Kelly as she went over to the desk and searched through a bundle of lab results that had just been delivered.

Kelly hesitated, wondering if she should try again to convince Letizia that she'd had no hand in the decision, but in the end she decided it wasn't worth it. Letizia would believe what she wanted to believe and there was no point wasting her time by trying to change her mind.

There was another clinic that afternoon so Kelly went straight to Outpatients after lunch. Fortunately, the list wasn't as long as the previous day's so she was finished well in time for the afternoon ward round. As usual Luca led the team and was as meticulous as ever. He left Chloe Robinson until the end so a good hour had passed by the time they gathered around her bed. The little girl was on intravenous antibiotics to fight off the infection plus a mild analgesic to make her more comfortable. Although Chloe looked a little brighter than when Kelly had seen her last, she knew there could still be problems with the child's kidneys. A twenty-four-hour kidney-function test had been requested and they would need to wait until they had the results of that before they would know for certain how badly her kidneys had been affected.

Luca frowned as he took Chloe's file from the ward sister. 'Where are the case notes?'

'They should be in there, *dottore,*' the sister assured him. She glanced uncertainly at Kelly. 'Dr Carlyon said that she was going to write them up after the patient was admitted.'

Luca shook his head. 'There's no sign of any notes in here.' He turned to Kelly. 'Keeping an accurate record is a basic requirement of the job, Dr Carlyon. I don't expect junior registrars to put off writing up notes until they feel like doing so. Please ensure that this file is brought up to date immediately.'

He handed Kelly the file then turned to Chloe's parents, giving her no opportunity to explain that she had written up the notes. She bit her lip when she saw the looks the rest of the group exchanged. They obviously believed that she had failed to do her job properly too, but it wasn't true.

Opening the file, she hurriedly checked its contents, but there was no sign of the notes she'd taken such care over writing. Was it possible that they'd fallen out and been placed in another patient's file by mistake? It seemed unlikely but it was the only explanation she could come up with. She would have to go through all the files and check.

As soon as the round finished, Kelly went to the office and systematically searched through every file in the cabinet but there was no sign of the notes she'd written. She knew she'd written them but, as she had no proof, there was no way to prove that she hadn't been negligent. The fact that Luca must now believe she wasn't capable of doing her job properly stung, but there was nothing she could do about it, apart from making sure that she didn't slip up again.

She sighed as she sat down at the desk. Even if she double-checked everything she did from now on, it might not be enough if he was looking for an excuse to get rid of her. Although he had claimed that he was happy to have her on his team, she must be a constant reminder to him of the past. Maybe he hadn't known that Sophia had been pregnant at the time, but he obviously felt guilty about their affair. The proof of that was the fact that he wanted nothing to do with her outside work. She could find that it wasn't solely up to her whether she stayed on here.

Luca went straight to his office after he left the ward. He had a meeting with the board the following day and he needed to prepare for it. Extra funding had been made available and he'd been asked to put forward a plan about how he wished to spend it. He was hoping to persuade the board to fund another senior registrar's post for his department. Although it would be costly to hire another senior doctor, the benefits would be enormous, and it was up to him to convince the board of that.

He skimmed through his notes, wanting to be sure that he had got his figures right. Although sometimes he grew impatient about the amount of paperwork that was involved, it was a necessary evil. Facts and figures needed to be written down so that mistakes weren't made. It was one of the basic tenets of medicine, which was why he'd been so surprised by Kelly's lapse. Was she really as good at her job as he'd thought she was, or was he allowing his personal feelings to influence his judgement?

It was worrying to think that he might have lost his objectivity. He prided himself on being an excellent judge of ability, but maybe he was wrong about Kelly. And if he was wrong about her then surely it changed things? He wouldn't need to worry so much about the harm he could cause to her career if he involved her in his affairs for a start.

Luca groaned when he realised that he was looking for excuses. It would be wrong of him to judge Kelly by one fairly minor blot on an otherwise spotless record. However, he would watch her more closely in the future, make sure that she really did live up to his expectations. It wasn't that he wanted her to fail, far from it. However, he was human enough to see the benefits if it happened.

His heart surged as pictures of the future they could have flooded his mind, before he blanked them out. Whatever happened, he would put Kelly's interests first.

It was late by the time Kelly finished her shift. Knowing that she had to be on her mettle put extra pressure on her and she found herself double-checking everything she did. It was gone seven when she left the hospital and headed to her apartment.

It was another glorious evening, the heat of the sun muted now to a pleasant warmth. She was loath to waste it by sitting indoors so as soon as she got in she showered and changed then set off to the harbour. She'd not made it to the restaurant the previous night. After her run-in with Luca she'd not felt like partying so she had phoned her friend and made her excuses. However, she intended to enjoy this evening even if she was on her own.

She took the same route down to the harbour, quickening her pace as she passed the villa so Luca wouldn't think she was loitering outside if he happened to see her. The gates were securely fastened that night so obviously he wasn't taking any chances of Matteo escaping again. She couldn't blame him. After losing his wife in such tragic circumstances, he must be terrified of anything happening to his son as well.

The thought of how Luca had suffered saddened her. Kelly couldn't rid herself of the image of him, grieving for the woman he had lost. Maybe he would meet someone else one day? Another woman with whom he could share his life and maybe have more children. They had often talked about the fact that they'd both wanted children one day, and Luca had made no secret of the fact that he was keen to be a father when the time was right. They'd even discussed what their children might look like: a dark-haired, grey eyed son—a miniature version of Luca—and a little girl with red hair and green eyes just like her.

Kelly's heart ached as the memory suddenly surfaced. She had schooled herself not to think about the past, but it was hard to chase away the images that filled her mind. Since she'd split up with Luca, she had been out with several other men, but she'd never wanted to have a child with any of them.

Bringing a child into the world was the ultimate commitment a man and a woman could make to each other, and their relationship needed to be rock-solid before they embarked on such a life-changing course. Kelly had seen how her own parents had struggled when she and her sister had been growing up. Having children had put an added strain on their already shaky marriage and in the end they had divorced.

She had sworn that she would never have a child unless she was certain it would have two loving parents, committed to raising it. That Luca had shared her views had thrilled her, but that had been before she'd found out about Sophia. Pain surged through her and for a moment she wondered if she should go back before she forced herself to carry on. She had to get on with her life, without Luca.

The restaurants around the harbour were busy with early evening diners. Sardinians loved children and there were lots of family groups eating out that night. Kelly checked a couple of the larger establishments but they were full so she decided to try one of the side streets instead. There were a number of small trattorias there which didn't attract as many tourists, but once again they were all full. She was ready to give up after she checked the last place and was told that there were no empty tables when she heard someone calling her name and when she looked round, she saw Luca waving to her from across the restaurant.

He got up and came over to her. 'If you're looking for a place to sit, there's room at our table.' He shrugged when she didn't say anything. 'We've almost finished so you can have the table to yourself after we leave.'

'That's very kind of you,' Kelly began, wondering how she could tactfully refuse. The last thing she needed at the present moment was to spend time with Luca when her emotions were so raw.

'It's common sense. You need somewhere to sit and we have a spare seat—problem solved.'

He seemed to have taken her agreement for granted as he made his way back to the table, but Kelly still hesitated. Maybe it was common sense but she wasn't as confident about handling this situation as he appeared to be.

She sighed when she saw him beckon imperiously to her. If she refused to sit with him then he would start to wonder what was wrong with her, and that was the last thing she wanted. His confidence in her had been shaken once that day and she needed to redress the damage as quickly as possible. If she was never going to have that family she had dreamed of, at least she would have her career so it was important that Luca continued to believe in her.

She took a deep breath then made her way across the restaurant. She had to do this for the sake of her career even if it was at the expense of her heart.

CHAPTER EIGHT

'AND I'll have a glass of red wine as well, please. The local house wine will be fine. *Grazie.*'

Luca waited while Kelly gave her order to the waiter. He still wasn't sure why he had insisted that she should sit with him and Matteo. Common sense dictated that he should have steered well clear of her, but for some reason he'd wanted to spend time with her. The thought worried him. He must never forget that he had to put Kelly's interests before his own.

'*Papà.*'

Luca started when Matteo demanded his attention. He smiled as the little boy held out his empty bowl to show him that he had finished all his pasta. 'Good boy,' he praised, ruffling his son's dark curls. 'Would you like some ice cream now?'

'*Sì. Sì.*' Matteo clapped his hands in delight, and Kelly laughed.

'I take it that he likes ice cream?'

'He loves it.' Luca summoned a smile, hoping she couldn't tell how on edge he felt. All he'd done had been to offer to share his table with her, he reminded himself sternly. There was no need to panic. 'If Matteo had his way, he would eat nothing except ice cream. I hate to admit it but I've had to do what so many parents do and resort to bribery to make sure he eats anything else.'

Kelly chuckled. 'It must have been a bitter blow to have to compromise your ideas on parenthood.'

Luca rolled his eyes. 'It certainly was. I always swore that I wouldn't resort to such tactics, but it's amazing how quickly your principles disappear when you're confronted with a stubborn two-year-old who refuses to eat.'

'A lot of children are faddy eaters at that age,' she pointed out, and he sighed.

'I know, but it's different when it's your child, believe me. All the facts and figures in the world don't mean a thing then.'

'It must be difficult for you.' She shrugged when he looked at her in surprise. 'I meant that it can't be easy bringing up a child on your own.'

'No, it isn't,' he said truthfully, because there was no point lying. 'I'm very aware that Matteo is missing out by not having his mother around. I try to make up for it as best I can, but it's not easy when I have to spend so much time apart from him.'

'Who looks after him while you're at work?'

'My housekeeper, Maria. She's been with me since Matteo was born and she adores him. However, I'm afraid it's becoming too much for her to look after him all the time,' he explained. 'Take last night, for instance, when he got out into the road. Maria was supposed to be watching him while he was playing in the garden, but she fell asleep. There'd been a delivery that afternoon and the gates hadn't been shut. Matteo must have seen his chance and took off. Heaven knows what would have happened if you hadn't been there.'

'It's impossible to watch a child twenty-four hours a day.'

'Yes, I know you're right, but it was a risk that could have been avoided with a little more care.'

'So what are you going to do? Are you going to hire a nanny to look after him if it's becoming too much for Maria to do it?'

Luca grimaced. 'I've tried that and it didn't work. The first girl I employed only stayed for a week. The next nanny I hired lasted a bit longer. She was with us for two months and she might have stayed even longer if I hadn't come home early one day and found Matteo screaming in his cot. He was soaking wet because his nappy hadn't been changed and he was desperate for a drink. Apparently, the nanny had spent the day by the swimming pool and hadn't bothered to check on him.'

'Oh, how awful.' Reaching out she ran a gentle hand over the little boy's curls. 'How could anyone do that?'

Luca felt his heart contract when he saw the concern on her face. He had to make a concerted effort not to show how much it had moved him. 'I didn't bother asking her. I sacked her on the spot and that was the last I saw of her. I couldn't face hiring anyone else in case the same thing happened again so I asked Maria if she would look after him. It's worked out really well so far, but now that Matteo is more mobile, Maria is struggling to cope. Keeping up with a lively two-year-old is a lot for a woman of her age.'

'Isn't there a crèche at the hospital?' she asked. 'One of the nurses mentioned it the other day, she said her little girl loves going there. Why don't you think about enrolling Matteo?'

'I don't think it would be suitable for him,' he said flatly.

'Why ever not? It would do him good to have other children to play with, plus it would mean that you could see him at lunchtime. It seems like the ideal solution to me.'

'Maybe it does, but you don't know Matteo like I do.'

Her face immediately closed up when she heard the bite in his voice. 'I apologise. I didn't mean to interfere.'

Luca sighed. He could tell that she was hurt and it was the last thing he'd intended. 'You aren't interfering, Kelly. I just feel that Matteo is better off at home to make up for the fact that I can't be with him for so much of the time.'

'I can understand that, really I can.' She leant forward and he could see the urgency in her eyes. His heart overflowed because he had never expected her to care about his problems after what had happened between them.

'However, I honestly believe that you don't have to be with a child all the time for him to feel secure. Katie and I were never sent to a nursery. Mum stayed at home when we were small and looked after us, yet I don't think we ever felt really secure. There was too much tension in the house because of the constant rows between our parents. It was a relief when they split up, in fact. At least they weren't arguing all the time then.'

Luca frowned. It was the first time she'd mentioned her parents, apart from when she'd told him briefly they were both dead. 'You never told me any of that before.'

'It never cropped up.' She shrugged, although he could tell that there was more to it than that. Had the events of her childhood had as much influence on her as his childhood had had on him? he wondered.

He still bore the scars of his past to this day and he always would. The brutal and uncaring regime at the children's home had left him with a deep-seated mistrust of authority. Even his reluctance to send Matteo to the crèche stemmed from his fear of handing over his son into the care of strangers.

He knew how it felt to be abandoned and helpless. He'd been six years old when his mother had left him at the home, and he could still recall the desolation he'd felt then, the sense of worthlessness which had been made worse by the attitude of the staff who had run the place. The physical abuse he had suffered there had been nothing compared to the psychological damage of knowing that he'd been unwanted.

He had always envied those people who had been brought up in their own homes by their parents, yet it didn't appear that Kelly's childhood had been particularly happy. Maybe it needed more than just a home environment to make a child feel secure?

It was unsettling to think that he might have been wrong so he was glad when the waiter arrived with Kelly's order. By the time the dishes had been arranged on the table and the wine poured, he felt more able to cope. Matteo's ice cream had arrived as well but the little boy pushed his hand away when he tried to help him scoop some onto his spoon.

Kelly laughed. 'I don't think he needs any help. He seems to be a dab hand with a spoon.'

'Especially if there's ice cream on the end of it,' Luca agreed, dryly. He tried to wipe a smear of ice cream off the child's chin then held up his hands when Matteo noisily protested. 'I'm sorry, *caro*. Am I getting in your way? Maybe I'd better leave the cleaning up until after you've finished.'

Tossing the napkin onto the table, he sat back in his seat. 'How's the pasta?' he asked as Kelly turned her attention to her own meal.

'Delicious. I wish I could make pasta this good.'

'There is a definite art to it,' he agreed.

'Hmm.' She twirled up another forkful and smiled at him. 'Did your mother teach you the secret of making perfect pasta, or didn't she believe that boys should have to cook for themselves?'

'I can't remember my mother ever cooking me a meal,' he said bluntly.

'Really?' Her brows rose. 'So who did the cooking in your house? Your father?'

'No. I never met my father. My parents weren't married so I lived with my mother until I was six and then I was put into care.'

'You mean that your mother died?' she said uncertainly.

'No.' He shook his head, wondering why he had told her that. He never spoke about his past. The only person who had known about it had been Sophia and that had been because she had been in a similar situation. The difference was that Sophia's parents had been killed in an accident, whereas his hadn't wanted him. Pain gripped him and he laughed harshly.

'My mother decided that she didn't want to look after me any more. She never made any secret of the fact that she would have had an abortion if she could have afforded it. I don't think a day went by, in fact, when she didn't tell me that she wished I hadn't been born. In the end, she did the next best thing—she put me in a home and forgot about me.'

Kelly didn't know what to say. She had never imagined that Luca had had such a terrible start in life. She opened her mouth then closed it again because anything she could think of would only sound trite. Anyway, what could she say to make him feel better? He didn't want her sympathy. He didn't want anything at all from her.

The thought brought a rush of tears to her eyes and he sighed. 'I'm sorry, Kelly. I didn't mean to upset you. The past is over and done with and there's really no point dwelling on it.'

'I wish you'd told me about it before.' She looked up, unable to keep the pain out of her eyes. 'It could have helped if you'd shared it with me, Luca.'

Something crossed his face, an expression of longing that startled her, before his face closed up again. 'Sophia knew all about my childhood. I was able to confide in her.'

Kelly recoiled at the deliberate rebuff. That he had felt able to share the details of his childhood with Sophia and not with her made her see how little he had cared about her. It took every scrap of strength she could muster not to let him see how hurt she felt. 'At least you had someone to talk to about what had gone on. I'm sure it must have helped.'

He inclined his head, although he didn't say anything. Kelly returned her attention to her meal but the food tasted like sawdust now. After a couple of mouthfuls she pushed the plate away. She picked up the glass, hoping the wine would help to numb the pain that was gnawing away inside her. It wasn't just the fact that Luca hadn't wanted her support that hurt, funnily enough, but the thought of how he must have suffered.

Tears welled to her eyes again as she looked at Matteo. Luca would have been just a few years older than his son when he'd been abandoned and she could imagine his bewilderment when his mother had left him with strangers. No wonder he was so determined to give Matteo a happy childhood.

'Don't.'

She started when a hand suddenly enfolded hers. Looking

up, she was stunned when she saw the regret in Luca's eyes. 'What do you mean?' she said shakily.

'You're upset because of what I told you and that's the last thing I want, Kelly. I don't want to involve you in my affairs. It isn't fair.'

'If you're worried that I'll get the wrong idea, there's no need.' She glared at him, desperate to convince him that she was telling the truth. 'I'm no more interested in us getting back together than you are, Luca. As far as I'm concerned, we're colleagues now and that's all we shall ever be.'

'Good. So long as we both understand the boundaries, we won't have a problem.'

He removed his hand and Kelly shivered when she was suddenly deprived of its warmth. It was a relief when he stood up and lifted Matteo out of the high-chair.

'It's time I took this little fellow home to bed. Enjoy the rest of your evening, Kelly.'

'Thank you. I shall.'

Kelly fixed a smile to her lips as he walked around the table. Matteo suddenly lunged towards her, his chubby little arms locking tightly around her neck, and instinctively she took him from Luca. The little boy pressed a sticky kiss on her cheek and beamed at her.

'*Ciao,*' he lisped.

'*Ciao* to you, Matteo,' she replied, kissing him back. She gave him a hug then lifted him up so that Luca could take him from her. Their hands touched and she bit back a gasp as a jolt of electricity scorched through her. She could feel herself trembling as Luca settled the little boy safely back in his arms, but oddly enough so was he.

Kelly's heart began to pound when she saw the tremors

that ran through his powerful body. In that moment she realised that everything he had told her had been a lie. He wasn't indifferent to her; he still cared about her. He may have married Sophia, but he still wanted her. And the proof of that was the passion she could see blazing in his eyes, a passion that was for her and her alone.

'I'll see you tomorrow, Kelly,' he said gruffly, swinging round.

Kelly didn't answer. She just sat and watched as he strode across the restaurant. He paid his bill then left without looking back and it was a relief because she had no idea what he would have seen on her face right then. Part of her was elated at the thought that he still wanted her whilst another part was afraid. She had sworn that she would never give anyone the opportunity to hurt her a second time, but the one thing she hadn't allowed for was that she would meet Luca again.

Panic swept through her as she summoned the waiter and asked him for her bill, only to be informed that the gentleman had already paid it. Kelly didn't argue; she merely gave the man a tip and left. She knew it would be silly to get upset because Luca had paid for her meal, and that she had to draw the line somewhere.

She couldn't allow Luca to take over her life again. After they had split up, she had lost all interest in everything, including her job. Work had been her driving force up till then. She had seen how her mother had struggled to earn a living after her parents had divorced and had sworn the same thing wouldn't happen to her, yet for almost a year she had lost sight of that and had coasted along. It had been her sister

Katie who had made her see that she had to pull herself together, and she had managed it in the end.

She had worked hard to make up for the time she'd lost and she was proud of the fact that she'd earned herself this prestigious post. Her life was back on track again and she would be a fool to risk ruining it a second time. It would be far safer if she maintained her distance from Luca from now on, but could she do it, or would temptation prove to be too strong?

Her heart caught as she recalled the expression on his face before he'd left. He may have claimed that he didn't want to involve her in his affairs, but she'd seen the passion in his eyes as well as the yearning. How could she be sure that Luca would be able to resist this attraction they felt for one another?

CHAPTER NINE

IT WAS barely seven a.m. when Luca arrived at the hospital the following morning. With his meeting with the board scheduled for nine o'clock, he'd wanted to get an early start. Fortunately, Matteo always woke up as soon as it was light so he'd been able to spend half an hour reading to him before he'd left. At least it had helped to stave off some of the guilt he felt about being absent for so long, although if what Kelly had said about children not needing their parents around all the time was true, maybe he shouldn't worry so much.

He sighed as he let himself into his office. He had spent the night thinking about Kelly and here he was thinking about her again this morning. Even when he had fallen asleep he had dreamt about her—erotic, disturbing dreams which had left him aching with frustration when he had woken up. Spending time with her last night had made him see how much he had missed her, but he had to conquer these feelings. He had his son to raise and a demanding job to do and there was no room in his life for her as well.

He had managed to get through quite a lot of work by the time his secretary buzzed to tell him that the team had arrived. He asked her to send them in, frowning when he discovered that Kelly was missing. Normally she was one of the first to arrive each day so he couldn't help worrying about what had happened to her.

'Where's Dr Carlyon?' he said curtly to hide his anxiety.

'I've no idea,' Carlo replied. 'She wasn't in the staff lounge.'

'Maybe she had a late night and overslept,' Letizia suggested, slyly.

'That is no excuse for not being here on time,' Luca stated tersely. He briefly explained that he had a meeting with the board, and that Carlo would be taking the morning ward round, then settled down to review a couple of cases. However, by the time they had worked their way halfway down the list, Kelly still hadn't appeared and he was growing increasingly concerned. He was just about to ask one of the housemen to go and see if she was in her apartment when she came into the office.

'I'm sorry I'm late,' she said, drawing up a chair. She didn't make any attempt to explain what had delayed her and Luca felt his temper flare. While he'd been sitting here, worrying himself to death, she'd been lying in bed.

He glared at her. 'I expect my staff to be here on time, Dr Carlyon. If they can't manage that then the very least I expect is that they send a message to let me know why they've been delayed. Perhaps you could make a note of that for future reference.'

A flush of colour touched her cheeks but she met his gaze. 'I apologise. It won't happen again, I assure you.'

Luca could tell that she was furious about the way he had spoken to her but he was in no mood to compromise. 'See that it doesn't,' he snapped.

The next hour flew past. Before he knew it, it was time to leave for the meeting with the board. He thanked everyone for their input and left his office. The meeting was being held in the boardroom so he made his way to the lift. It was extremely busy that morning and he was still waiting for the lift to arrive when his team passed him on their way to the ward. Kelly was at the back of the group and she ignored him as she stalked past.

Luca sighed. He knew that she was upset about the way he had spoken to her but he couldn't let her get away with being late—it wouldn't have been fair to the rest of the team. Anyway, she should have known better than to have kept everyone waiting.

The lift arrived but as he stepped inside, he found himself wondering once again if she really was as good at her job as he'd thought she was. In the past few days she'd made several basic errors and it was worrying to wonder if his belief in her had been misplaced. He would have to keep a close eye on what she was doing from now on and not just for the sake of their patients either. If she needed a guiding hand then he intended to be there for her. If she would let him.

Kelly was seething with anger as she followed the team to the ward. Despite what Luca believed, she had sent a message to explain that she might be late for the case meeting. She had no idea what had happened to it but that was less important than the fact that he'd seen fit to speak to her in such a fashion. He seemed to derive a positive pleasure from embarrassing her in front of her colleagues.

'Don't let it get you down, Kelly. Luca can be a bit sharp at times, but he's usually very fair.'

'I know.' Kelly summoned a smile when Carlo came over to her, not wanting him to suspect how hurt she felt. 'I must just rub him up the wrong way, I expect.'

'I think it's more a case of him being such a perfectionist.' Carlo laughed. 'He puts so much into his own job and he expects everyone else to do the same. He doesn't understand that we are just human beings and can only do our best.'

'I'm sure you're right,' she agreed, wishing it was that simple. Was it the guilt Luca felt about Sophia that drove him to be so hard on her? she wondered. It was the only explanation she could come up with, and it was worrying to wonder if the situation would continue. Luca obviously found it as difficult as she did to forget about the past so maybe she should accept that and leave. However, part of her was reluctant to give up a job she had dreamed about for so long.

'What happened this morning?' Carlo asked as they walked along the corridor. 'It's not like you to be late for a case meeting.'

'I wasn't late, actually,' Kelly explained. 'I was here just after seven and went to see how Chloe Robinson was doing. Her parents were really upset because she'd had a bad night so I took them for a cup of coffee. I did ask one of the nurses to send a message to Luca to say that I might be delayed, but it couldn't have reached him.'

Carlo stared at her in dismay. 'Why on earth didn't you tell him that?'

'Because he never gave me the chance.'

'Then I'll tell him. It's not fair that you should be blamed for being late when you were working.'

'It's really kind of you, Carlo, but I'd rather you didn't say anything.' She shrugged when he looked at her in surprise.

'It will only sound as though I'm trying to come up with an excuse and I don't want Luca thinking that. It's better if I forget about it and just make sure that I don't give him any more reasons to tell me off.'

'Well, if you're sure that's what you want,' Carlo said uncertainly.

'It is,' she said firmly, pushing open the ward door.

Thankfully, Carlo let the subject drop, although she could tell that he thought she was making a mistake. Maybe she was, but if Luca was intent on believing the worst of her, there was little she could do about it.

It was a depressing thought and Kelly found it very difficult to shrug off. Fortunately, she was kept so busy that she had no time to brood. As soon as they had finished the ward round they had two new admissions. Two-year-old twin boys, Stefano and Sebastiano, had been rushed to the hospital after suffering breathing difficulties. Carlo was rostered for clinic that morning and Letizia was writing up notes so it was left to Kelly to respond when Pronto Soccorso telephoned the ward.

She went straight down to the emergency department where she was met by a scene of chaos. It appeared that the twins were on holiday with their parents and their extended family. The department was full of aunts, uncles and cousins, and the noise they were making was dreadful.

Kelly bypassed the throng of relatives and made her way to the treatment room, smiling sympathetically at Magdalena Cavalli, the duty doctor, as she went in. 'Looks like you've been having fun down here.'

'I'm not sure if I would call it fun,' Magdalena retorted. 'The noise is giving me a headache and it's not helping the little ones either. They're getting more upset because they can hear people shouting. I've just asked the parents if they can go and calm everyone down.'

'Then the sooner we get the boys sorted out the better,' Kelly said as she approached the bed. The twins were lying side by side and it was immediately obvious that they were having problems breathing despite the oxygen they were receiving.

'Any history of asthma?' she asked, unlooping her stethoscope so she could listen to their chests. She warmed the end of the stethoscope in her hand then placed it against the first tiny chest, frowning when she heard crepitations—bubbling sounds—coming from the little boy's lungs.

'No. The parents claim that both boys have never had a day's illness since they were born,' Magdalena explained.

'And they've had all their vaccinations? They're given as standard during a child's first year throughout Europe, I believe.'

'That is correct and according to the parents the boys have completed the full course of vaccinations. We shall check on that when we receive copies of their medical notes from their own doctor. The family is from Rome so we've faxed a message through to the surgery and are waiting for a reply.'

'Good. At least we'll be able to rule out something like diphtheria if their vaccinations are up to date,' Kelly said in relief.

She checked the other twin and could hear the same bubbling noises coming from his lungs. His breathing was extremely rapid, too, and he appeared to have a fever. He was also coughing at intervals, as was his brother. Kelly frowned as she added up all the symptoms.

'I wonder if it could be bronchiolitis. The symptoms certainly fit. I think we should request a blood test to see if the respiratory syncytial virus is present.'

'I'll do an order for the lab,' Magdalena offered.

'Thanks. In the meantime, I'd like to admit them. They're obviously struggling and they'll need oxygen therapy. If the small airways are inflamed, they might benefit from physiotherapy, too, to help shift some of that mucus. Could you let the parents know?' She grinned. 'My Italian is probably not up to trying to answer that mob out there, I'm afraid.'

'Your Italian is better than you think it is,' Magdalena retorted. She laughed when Kelly pulled a face. 'All right, I'll explain it to them. I don't blame you for not wanting to get involved in that melee.'

'Thanks,' Kelly replied with a grin.

She left Magdalena to arrange the transfer and went back to the ward. By the time the twins were settled in it was lunchtime but once again she didn't bother taking a break. She went to the office instead and wrote up the boys' notes, double-checking that they were correctly filed before locking the filing-cabinet drawer. What with notes going missing and messages not being delivered, she seemed to be jinxed and she was determined that Luca wouldn't have any more reason to find fault with her that day.

Luca was glad to get the meeting over. Although the board had agreed to fund another senior registrar's post, he'd found it difficult to remain focused. He'd kept wondering if he'd been too harsh with Kelly, and that had put him off his stride. It wasn't easy treating her as just another colleague, as he was discovering to his cost. He wasn't sure what the solution was but they had to find a way to work together without it causing so much upheaval.

He went straight to the office as soon as he arrived back at the ward. Having missed the ward round, he wanted to check on the progress of a couple of the children. Although he knew that he could trust Carlo to deal with things in his absence, he preferred to keep his finger firmly on the pulse. Opening the door, he went to step into the room then stopped dead when he saw Kelly standing beside the filing cabinet.

All of a sudden his heart began to race. For the past two years he had done his best to forget about her but he had failed. She was imprinted on his heart, etched into his brain, and nothing he did could alter that. She was his soul-mate, his other half, the one person who could make him whole. In that moment he knew that he would regret it for the rest of his life if he didn't tell her that, but could he do it? Did he have the right to tell her that he loved her when, ultimately, it might destroy everything she held dear?

CHAPTER TEN

'OH, I DIDN'T hear you come in.' Kelly could feel her cheeks burning as she turned away from the filing cabinet and saw Luca standing in the doorway. She cleared her throat, hoping he couldn't tell how nervous she felt. Although after what had happened that morning, it was understandable if she felt on edge around him. 'Were you looking for me?'

'No. I just wanted to check on a couple of patients,' he explained, coming into the room.

'I see.' Kelly dredged up a smile but there was something about the way he was looking at her that made her feel even more flustered. 'As long as you haven't come to tell me off again, that's all right.'

His eyes darkened. 'Meaning that you feel I have been too hard on you recently?'

'I suppose so,' she admitted reluctantly, wishing that she hadn't said anything. She didn't want him thinking that she was complaining about the treatment she'd received. After all, as far as Luca was concerned, she deserved to be taken to task about the missing notes and being late. However, it still rankled to know that he had so little faith in her.

'Then I can only apologise.' His voice dropped, the deep

tones grating slightly. 'I never meant to upset you, Kelly. It's the last thing I wanted to do.'

'And I didn't mean to upset you either, Luca.' She hesitated, unsure whether she should say this, but it was too important to withhold the truth. 'I care about you far too much.'

'I care about you, too. Maybe that's why we've been finding it so hard when we're at work. It isn't easy dealing with our feelings, is it?'

'No. I try not to think about the past, but I can't just dismiss it either. You and I had an affair, Luca, and we can't ignore that fact no matter how much we might want to do so.'

'So what do you suggest?'

'I don't know, but this obviously isn't working for either of us, is it?'

'What if we allowed ourselves to become friends as well as colleagues?' he suggested slowly. 'Do you think we'd find it less of a strain then?'

'I'm not sure. Possibly.' She frowned as she tested out the idea of being Luca's friend. It would be better than what they had, but would it be enough, or would she ultimately find herself wanting more than friendship from him?

The thought worried her and she hurried on. 'We can try it and see how it goes. After all, we have nothing to lose, do we?'

'Nothing at all.' He gave her a quick smile and her heart turned over when she saw the warmth in his eyes. It was all she could do not to melt into his arms, only she didn't think that friendship extended that far.

'So, now we have established that we're going to try to get along better, how do you feel about spending some time with me and Matteo this weekend?'

'What do you have in mind?' she said cautiously, wondering if she was leaping out of the proverbial frying-pan into the very heart of the fire.

'Oh, something really low-key that friends enjoy doing together.' He laughed. 'Don't look so scared. I was thinking along the lines of a picnic on the beach followed by a session of building sandcastles. It would be perfect for our first outing as friends, although I should warn you that I am an expert when it comes to beach architecture. I won't suggest that we have a competition because I know that I'll win.'

'Oh, really?' She gave him a frosty look, although it was hard not to laugh at such a preposterous claim. 'Sure you're not being a touch overconfident, Dr Ferrero? I'm a dab hand at making sand pies myself, I'll have you know.'

'Phoof.' He waved a dismissive hand. 'Sand pies are for amateurs. I'm talking about real castles with moats and water flowing through them.'

'And you don't believe my skills could ever match yours?' she said silkily. 'Hmm, we'll see about that. You could be in for a nasty shock.'

She laughed up at him, feeling happier than she'd felt since she'd arrived on the island. She hadn't realised what a strain it had been to keep him at a distance all the time. Maybe he was right to suggest that they should try to be friends from now on. At least it meant they could spend some time together and that would help to fill the gap he had left in her life when he'd left her.

Kelly caught herself up short. She had to forget about what they'd meant to each other in the past and focus on their new relationship. She smiled as she held out her hand. 'Here's to friendship—let's shake on it.'

'For ever friends,' he agreed, taking her hand.

Kelly felt her breath catch as his fingers closed around hers. Ripples of sensation were racing from her fingertips and spreading through her whole body. She was immediately transported back in time. Whenever Luca had touched her then, she'd felt exactly the same, as though her whole body were charged with energy, and it was alarming to know that he could have the same devastating effect even now. It was a relief when he released her.

'I'd better make a start on reading those notes,' he explained as he went to the desk.

'And I'd better get some work done before you think I'm slacking,' she said quickly.

'I have never thought that of you, Kelly,' he said firmly. 'I know how much effort you always put into your work.'

'Thank you. That means a lot to me.' She gave him a quick smile then hurried to the door before she was tempted to linger any longer. Even friendship came with boundaries and she had no intention of crossing them at such an early stage. 'I'll see you at the afternoon ward round, I expect.'

'*Si.*'

He didn't say anything else as he pulled out a chair and sat down. Kelly left the office and went back to the ward and checked on the twins. She had a word with their parents and assured them that the boys weren't in any immediate danger then phoned the lab and chased up their test results.

The lab technician promised to get them back by the morning so she had to be content with that. And at least she knew that the boys were receiving the very best care available. The Santa Margherita Ospedale was renowned throughout Europe and the experience she gained there would stand her in good stead in the future. Slowly but surely she was moving towards where she wanted to end up—as a professor of paediatric care at a major teaching hospital where she could pass on her knowledge to others. It was the job she had dreamed about since she'd been a teenager and it was within her grasp if she did well here. The hospital's reputation was such that any application she made in the future would be looked upon favourably, which was why she was so glad that she and Luca had found a solution to their problems at last. From now on they were going to be friends as well as colleagues, and that would surely help to ease the pain of not having any other role in his life.

He must have been mad! As Luca started packing the picnic hamper, he could feel panic rising inside him. He could scarcely believe that he'd been rash enough to suggest that Kelly should accompany him and Matteo to the beach. Did he honestly believe he would be able to stick to those claims he'd made about them being friends? Like hell he could!

He groaned. It wasn't friendship he wanted from Kelly. It was a hell of a lot more than that so why was he putting himself through this torment? He should telephone her and cancel the outing before he made a complete fool of himself.

He left the kitchen and headed across the hall then stopped dead when he heard the doorbell ring. Glancing at his watch, he realised with a sinking heart that it had to be Kelly. He felt like a condemned man must feel as he made his way to the door, but he had to snap out of it. *He* had organised this outing and *he* would have to deal with the fallout from it.

Luca took a deep breath and opened the door. '*Buongiorno,* Kelly. You're nice and early.'

'Not too early, I hope,' she said, uncertainly.

Luca sighed when he saw the discomfort on her face. It wasn't fair to make her feel uncomfortable because he had doubts about the wisdom of what he was doing. 'Of course not,' he said firmly, ushering her inside. He led her to the kitchen, waving a hand towards the hamper. 'I'm in the process of packing our lunch, although from the amount of food Maria has prepared for us, she obviously thinks we'll be gone for a week.'

'You could feed a small army with this lot,' Kelly agreed.

Luca felt his senses whirl when she smiled at him. She looked so beautiful that he longed to take her in his arms and kiss her, only it wasn't the sort of thing a friend would do. 'You certainly could,' he said, struggling to inject a little levity into his voice. 'However, if I dare to leave anything behind, Maria will start sulking.'

He quickly packed the remaining items into the hamper, using the few seconds it took to get himself in hand. He had to start as he meant to go on if this day wasn't going to turn into a complete disaster.

'Right, I think that's everything,' he said, lifting the basket off the table. 'I'll just put this in the car then fetch Matteo.'

'Where is he?' Kelly asked, glancing around.

'He's in the garden. I thought it best to keep him occupied while I got everything ready.' He summoned a smile, hoping it didn't look as strained as it felt. 'He gets very excited when he knows we're going to the beach, and makes himself sick.'

'Oh, the poor little love!' she exclaimed.

Luca felt his heart ache when he saw the concern in her eyes. He quickly excused himself and went out to the car. There was no point torturing himself with the thought of what a wonderful mother she would make. If Kelly decided to have a family one day, it wouldn't be his child that she lavished all that love on but some other guy's.

CHAPTER ELEVEN

KELLY could feel her tension rising as they drove away from the villa. She knew they had to establish some kind of a relationship if they were to work together, but would friendship be enough? Her heart hiccuped as she stole a glance at Luca's handsome profile because it wasn't going to be easy to confine her feelings within such narrow boundaries.

'I thought we'd go to a little cove I discovered not long after I moved here. It's a bit off the beaten track so it tends to be quieter there.'

Luca took his eyes off the road for a second and Kelly hastily smoothed her features into a suitably bland expression. 'Sounds good to me. It gets so busy around the harbour, especially at the weekend.'

'A lot of Italians own second homes in Sardinia,' he explained, turning his attention back to the road. 'They fly out on a Friday night and spend the weekend here, and that's what bumps up the population.'

'Plus there's all the tourists who visit the island,' she said, happy to forget about her problems for the moment. 'It must have changed the whole nature of the place once mass tourism took off.'

'I'm sure it did. I know I've seen a lot of changes in the short time I've lived here,' he agreed, turning off the main road onto a narrow track. They were skirting the edge of the cliffs now and Kelly gulped when she saw the steep drop below.

'Really?' she said, hoping he couldn't see that she was gripping tight hold of her seat.

'Relax. You're quite safe.' He treated her to a tender smile. 'I wouldn't have brought you this way if I thought I was putting you and Matteo in any danger, Kelly.'

'Take no notice of me.' Kelly tried to smooth the wobble out of her voice, although it wasn't fear that had put it there. It was the way Luca had smiled at her. Had it been a ploy to reassure a nervous passenger, or had it been a sign that he still had feelings for her?

'I've always had a thing about heights,' she said hastily, not wanting to go down that route. 'I can't even climb on a chair without feeling dizzy.'

'I never knew that.' He swung the car through a narrow opening and stopped. Once again, Kelly was struck by the concern in his eyes as he turned to her.

'It must never have cropped up before,' she said lightly, deliberately glancing out of the window.

Why was Luca so intent on keeping her at a distance if he still had feelings for her? she wondered. She longed to ask him yet she knew how dangerous it would be to force him to explain. It would make it even more difficult for them to work together if she put him on the spot, and it could mean that she would have to quit her job. The thought of having to explain to a future employer why she had left a position most registrars would give their right arm for made her feel sick.

It could cause irreparable damage to her career and she didn't think she could cope with that, with losing Luca and her career all over again.

'Is this where we're going to have our picnic?' she said, swiftly changing the subject.

'That's right.'

Thankfully, Luca took his cue from her. Opening the car door, he got out and unfastened Matteo's safety harness. He lifted him out of the car and crouched down in front of him. 'Remember what *Papà* told you the last time we came here, *caro?* You are to hold my hand and not go running off because the path is very steep.'

'And I could fall over and hurt myself,' Matteo said seriously.

'*Si.* You remembered what I told you. Good boy.'

Kelly felt a lump come to her throat as she watched Luca tousle his son's hair. He was such a wonderful father to the little boy, but she'd always known he would be. Pain lanced through her and she turned away. There was no point dwelling on the thought that once she had believed that his children would be hers as well. Walking round to the boot, she started to unload the buckets and spades, summoning a smile when he came to help her because she couldn't bear it if he knew how devastated she felt.

'I'll take the picnic hamper,' he told her. He grimaced as he lifted it out of the car. 'It feels as though it's filled with lead weights.'

'We'll have to make sure we eat everything so we don't have to carry it back up the path,' she said with a rather shaky laugh.

'Are you all right?'

Luca put the hamper on the ground and looked at her in concern, but Kelly had no intention of telling him what was wrong. 'Fine,' she said breezily. She picked up one of the bags then grinned at him. 'I'm looking forward to today. I'm going to enjoy beating you at your own game.'

His brows rose. 'My own game?'

'Mmm, beach architecture was what you very grandiosely called it, I believe.' She took the travel rug out of the boot, smiling as though she hadn't a care in the world. 'It's time you had your comeuppance, Dr Ferrero, and I'm just the woman to make it happen.'

He chuckled as he closed the boot lid. 'I'm not sure I understand exactly what comeuppance means, but I can guess. Don't get too carried away, though. It takes years of practice to reach my level of expertise.'

'Oh, really!' Kelly hooted with laughter. 'We'll soon see about that!'

Luca sighed theatrically. 'I just hope you aren't too disappointed when you lose, Kelly.'

'Lose? The word's not in my vocabulary.' She gave him another smile, feeling easier now they were on safer ground. It was when they touched on the past that it became difficult, but she would learn to deal with the memories somehow. 'I'm so confident, in fact, that I'll have a wager with you: the loser buys dinner.'

'I never say no to a free meal.'

'Oh, *puhlease!* If that was an attempt to psyche me out then you're going to have to try harder than that.' She held out her hand. 'So is it a deal, then?'

'Oh, yes, although I do hate to take your hard-earned money.'

He laughed as he shook her hand. Kelly smiled back, hoping he couldn't feel how fast her pulse was racing. Picking up another one of the bags, she set off down the path. She could hear Matteo chattering away as he skipped along behind her and the deeper rumble of Luca's voice as he replied. Tears welled to her eyes because, to anyone watching, it would appear that they were a proper family enjoying a day out, but they would be wrong. She wasn't part of this family and she never would be. There was no place for her in either the father's or the son's heart.

'Now you have to bang your spade on the bottom of the bucket…that's right.'

Luca laughed as Matteo vigorously attacked the bucket. The day seemed to be going really well after rather a shaky start. Kelly had joined in with all the games, although he had sensed a certain sadness beneath her laughter. He sighed as he watched her help Matteo tip up his bucket. He hated to think that he was responsible for her unhappiness, even though there was little he could do about it. He couldn't overstep the bounds of friendship by asking too many questions.

'Look, *Papà*.'

Matteo's shrill little voice claimed his attention and he smiled when he saw the perfect sand pie his son had made. 'That is wonderful, Matteo. It's the best sand pie I've ever seen.'

He gave him a hug, delighting in his achievement. It was at moments like this when he wished that Sophia could have been there to see how well her beloved child was doing. It seemed unutterably cruel that she had been denied this joy after all she had suffered.

The thought sent a rush of emotion flooding through him but he forced it down. He couldn't afford to become emotional today of all days. Having Kelly around was already taxing his self-control, without adding to the stress. He summoned a smile as he turned to her, determined to keep the mood as upbeat as possible.

'How about we have our contest after lunch? Matteo usually has a nap then so it would be the best time if you're still up for it.'

'Oh, I never back out of a challenge,' she declared with a grin. She brushed the sand off her hands and stood up. 'I'll go and unpack the picnic.'

Luca watched her walk over to where they had left the hamper. She had taken off her jeans and T-shirt as soon as they'd got to the beach to reveal a black, one-piece swimsuit underneath. Although it was modestly cut, he'd had the devil's own job keeping his eyes off her. Even now, he could feel his body quicken as he took stock of the slender lines of her figure and hurriedly leapt to his feet. He needed something to distract him and there was nobody better qualified to do that than his son.

'How about another dip in the sea before we have our lunch?' he suggested, holding out his hand.

'*Si, si!*' Matteo slipped his hand into his father's then hesitated when he realised that Kelly wasn't going with them. 'Isn't Kelly coming?' he demanded.

'I'm not sure if she wants to come with us this time,' Luca replied. He turned to Kelly and quickly relayed the question. 'Matteo wants to know if you're coming into the water with us.'

'I think I'll give it a miss this time,' she said, smiling at the little boy. 'I'll get lunch ready while you two have a paddle.'

Luca led the little boy to the water. They splashed around for a while but it was obvious the child's heart wasn't in it. As soon as they got out, Matteo went scampering back up the beach to find Kelly. Luca sighed as he followed him. It seemed that Kelly had worked her magic on his son as well as on him. He could only hope that Matteo wouldn't be too upset when she left.

It was a sobering thought and he knew that he would have to give it some thought. However, now really wasn't the time to worry about it. He towelled himself dry then sat down on the edge of the rug.

'I'm not sure where to begin,' he said ruefully, eyeing the numerous dishes. There were pieces of crispy chicken coated in herbs; slices of ham; *bottariga*—salted, dried fish roe; *panadas*—small cylindrical pies filled with meat and vegetables; plus a selection of local sweets like *sebadas*—ravioli-like pastries filled with cheese and covered with honey.

'I'd just dive in and not worry about it,' Kelly advised him, helping herself to a *panada*. She cut it in two then offered half to Matteo. 'Do you want a piece of this, darling?' she asked him.

The little boy nodded eagerly as she handed it to him. She helped him take a bite then wiped some bits of pastry off his chin. It was all done so naturally that Luca felt his heart bunch up inside him. He quickly helped himself to some of the food. He had to stop thinking about what a wonderful mother she would make and concentrate on what was really important. And the most important thing of all was making sure that Kelly achieved her dreams.

Half an hour later, they had eaten their fill. While Kelly packed the remains of the picnic into the hamper, Luca settled Matteo down for his nap. Kelly smiled when Luca went back to her a few minutes later.

'That was quick. He must be worn out, the poor little love.'

'He is.' Luca took a deep breath as he felt his heart spasm again. Maybe Kelly did genuinely care about Matteo, but he couldn't afford to involve her in his affairs when she needed to concentrate on her career. 'He usually sleeps for about an hour after lunch so we should have time to build those sand-castles if you're still game.'

'I most definitely am.' She picked up a bright red bucket and spade. 'I'm not letting you weasel your way out of paying for dinner.'

Luca laughed as he picked up a spade. 'To the winner the spoils.'

They each chose a section of the beach close to the water and set to work. Luca worked methodically, building each part of the castle in turn. During his time at university he'd supplemented his grant by working as a waiter at one of Italy's most popular holiday resorts. He'd needed every penny he'd earned so he'd spent most of his free time at the beach and that was where he had developed his skills. They stood him in good stead because the castle soon took shape. Once the ramparts were finished, he added the turrets and a moat then dug a trench leading to the sea. Water soon began to trickle along it and in no time at all the castle was surrounded by water. Dusting the sand off his hands, he glanced over at Kelly and grinned when he saw that part of her castle was already listing dangerously to one side.

'That thing looks as though it's ready to collapse,' he jeered.

'Rubbish! It's as strong as yours is,' she retorted, then gasped in dismay when one wall of her castle suddenly gave way.

Luca couldn't help himself. The expression on her beautiful face was so comical that he burst out laughing. 'I think I win, don't you?' he said, grinning from ear to ear.

'Knowing you, Luca Ferrero, you probably sabotaged it,' she muttered, kicking a chunk off the offending wall.

'Now, now, don't be a sore loser,' he admonished. 'I did warn you I was a master at building sandcastles.'

'So you did. It must be a huge comfort to know that you're right all the time.'

'I wish I was, but I'm afraid I make as many mistakes as the next person does.'

Luca wasn't sure why he had said that, or at least not in *that* tone. He felt himself tense when Kelly stared at him. 'What sort of mistakes have you ever made?' she said in a taut little voice.

'Far too many to list.'

He gave her a quick smile then bent to pick up the spade, feeling his heart aching. The biggest mistake he'd made had been letting her go, but he couldn't tell her that when it would mean him telling her about Sophia and Matteo as well. He had sworn that he would never reveal the truth about Matteo's birth, and he couldn't go back on his word.

'Everyone makes mistakes, Luca, but it doesn't mean they can't make amends if they really want to.'

Luca's breath caught. He understood what she was saying. She was telling him that he could make up for the mistakes he'd made, too. The fact that she was willing to forgive him touched him deeply.

'I don't think it's possible to rewrite history,' he said harshly, afraid that temptation would get the better of him. It wasn't just the fear of breaking his promise that worried him but the damage it could cause if he told Kelly the truth. He mustn't lose sight of the fact that he needed to maintain his distance from her to safeguard her career.

'That wasn't what I meant.' All of sudden she was standing in front of him and he could see the plea in her eyes. When she laid her hand on his arm, he froze. He knew that he should stop what was happening yet he couldn't seem to move. All he could do was stand there as she continued in the same urgent tone.

'Nobody should try to rewrite their past because it's what makes us who we are. Sophia was a huge part of your life, Luca, and I understand that.'

All of a sudden common sense reasserted itself. He had hurt her enough already without making matters worse by having to rebuff her attempts at a reconciliation. 'I really don't think we should be having this conversation,' he said flatly.

'I'm sure you're right. But I can't help how I feel, Luca—can you?'

There were tears in her eyes now and he realised in that moment that he was lost. Reaching out, he pulled her into his arms, needing the feel of her heart beating beneath his to erase some of the agony he felt. His life had been so empty without her. Even though he was surrounded by people every single day, he always felt alone. But when he was with her, he didn't need anyone else. He just needed her. She was enough to heal the pain of the past, and more than enough to fill his future with happiness.

The thought tipped him over the edge as common sense buckled beneath the magnitude of his need for her. Bending, he kissed her with a hunger he couldn't hide and felt her respond with equal fervour. Their mouths meshed as though they were both desperate for the contact. Whole minutes passed and still they clung to each other as though neither was prepared to let the other one go. It took a supreme effort of will to draw back and he almost faltered when he saw the hunger in her eyes.

Kelly wanted him as much as he wanted her so why was he denying them what their hearts yearned for? If he told her how he really felt, that he loved her and that he had never stopped loving her, they could spend the rest of their lives together…

'Papà!'

The shrill little cry jolted him back to reality with sickening speed. Kelly didn't say a word as he let her go and hurried up the beach. He picked Matteo up and cuddled him close. He knew that Kelly had followed him but he didn't look at her. He focused on his son instead, on his responsibilities, and on his future.

Tears burned his eyes but he wouldn't cry. The last time he'd cried had been the day his mother had left him at the children's home and he'd not shed a tear since then. Tears didn't achieve anything, as he had discovered. They didn't make things better and they didn't ease the pain. He had no time for tears when he had a child to raise.

He took a steadying breath then turned to Kelly. She looked extremely pale but she seemed composed enough and he was relieved about that. He couldn't have stood it if she'd looked as upset as he himself felt. 'That should never have happened, and I apologise for it.'

'I apologise too. I overstepped the line just now, Luca, but it won't happen again.'

She didn't say anything else as she picked up the rug. Luca wished that he could think of something else to say that would make the situation right between them but it was impossible. They had stepped beyond the bounds of friendship with that kiss and there could be no going back.

Tears burned his eyes again but once again he refused to let them fall. Grown men didn't cry—they bore their pain stoically and without any fuss. That would be his mantra for however long Kelly remained in Sardinia, although what would happen after she left was something he didn't dare contemplate. Looking towards the lonely future which lay ahead could prove to be a step too far.

CHAPTER TWELVE

'ALESSANDRO can go home after lunch. Can you contact his parents and let them know, please?'

It was Monday morning and Kelly was in the process of sorting out which of the children were being discharged that day. Alessandro Alessi was first on her list so she ticked off his name. There were three more children who were well enough to go home so she made sure the ward sister had a note of their names then went to the office. Once she had finished all the necessary paperwork, she would need to get ready for the weekly team meeting. Quite frankly, she was dreading it. What on earth had possessed her to throw herself at Luca that way?

Kelly's mouth compressed as she sat down at the desk. She had spent the rest of Saturday and all day Sunday worrying about what had happened, but it hadn't achieved anything. The truth was that she had made a fool of herself and now she would have to suffer the consequences. She quickly filled in the discharge forms and printed out letters to be sent to each child's family doctor. She had just finished when there was a knock on the door and when she looked up she found Mr and Mrs Robinson standing outside.

'Hello, what I can I do for you?' she said, getting up.

'We were wondering what time Chloe is being discharged,' Wendy explained. 'We heard the sister telling some of the other parents they can take their children home after lunch but nobody has said anything about when Chloe can leave.'

'I don't think Dr Ferrero has decided when he will discharge her yet,' Kelly explained as she went over to the filing cabinet. It was news to her that the girl would be leaving hospital so soon, but maybe Luca had decided that she was well enough to be discharged. Pulling out Chloe's file, she checked her notes.

The results of the kidney-function test had shown a definite rise in the levels of urea and creatinine in Chloe's blood. Both substances were normally eliminated from the body by the kidneys so it was an indication the child's kidneys weren't functioning properly. A creatinine clearance test had also been carried out. This test compared the amount of creatinine in the blood with the amount in the urine over a period of twenty-four hours and it, too, indicated that Chloe's kidneys weren't working as well as they should have been doing.

Kelly put the file on the desk and invited the parents to sit down. 'I'm not sure where you got the idea that Chloe would be leaving us today but I'm afraid it isn't true. The tests we carried out over the weekend show that her kidneys are still in need of support. It would be extremely dangerous to remove her from hospital at the present time.'

'But we were told that Chloe would be well enough to go home today,' Mr Robinson protested, looking less than pleased.

Kelly's heart sank. There was nothing more distressing for the parents than to be told one thing by one doctor and something different by another. 'I'm not sure how it happened, but I'm afraid you were given the wrong information. Chloe will need to stay here until we're sure her kidneys are functioning properly.'

'Well, I'm not at all happy about this, I can tell you.' John Robinson glared at her. 'I booked our flights home on the strength of what I was told and now I'm going to have to cancel them again.'

'I really am very sorry,' Kelly apologised. 'Obviously, there's been a misunderstanding, but Chloe definitely won't be discharged today.'

'So when exactly will she be fit enough to leave?' Wendy demanded.

'That's something I can't tell you yet. All I can say is that as soon as we feel it is safe for Chloe to be discharged, we will let you know immediately.'

Kelly could tell that Mr and Mrs Robinson were far from happy when they left the office and she couldn't blame them, either. She read through Chloe's notes again but there was nothing written in them to say who had told them their daughter would be discharged that day.

She cleared everything away then made her way to the residents' lounge for a cup of coffee before the meeting began. Carlo was in there and he was as mystified as she was when she told him what had gone on. Although he had been on duty over the weekend, he certainly hadn't given instructions that Chloe could be discharged.

'What about Letizia?' Kelly suggested. 'She was working over the weekend so do you think it's possible that she took it upon herself to tell the parents that Chloe could go home today?'

'I wouldn't put it past her.' Carlo sighed. 'It's just the sort of thing she'd do, in fact. She has such an inflated opinion of her own capabilities.'

'Maybe you could have a word with her and check?' Kelly grimaced. 'If I say anything to her, all hell will break out. She and I don't seem to have hit it off, I'm afraid.'

'Probably because Letizia knows you are by far the better doctor.' Carlo smiled at her. 'She's not the sort of person who enjoys being second best, and especially not when there's a promotion in the offing.'

'Promotion?' Kelly echoed in surprise. 'Nobody mentioned it to me.'

'I only found out myself on Friday. Apparently, the board has authorised another senior registrar's post for our department. Play your cards right and you could be in the running for it, Kelly.'

Kelly frowned as Carlo went away to pour himself another cup of coffee. She'd had no idea that the board were thinking of funding another senior post. Just for a moment she allowed herself the luxury of imagining what would happen if she was lucky enough to be offered the job. It would be a definite step up the career ladder towards where she wanted to end up.

She sighed when it struck her how unlikely it was that she would be considered for the post. The job would go to someone with far more experience, and someone who intended to stay. After what had happened on Saturday, it seemed less likely than ever that she would be staying on here.

* * *

Luca could feel tension humming away inside him as he headed to his office for the weekly team meeting. He'd managed to avoid Kelly up till now because he'd had an early clinic, but he couldn't put off seeing her for much longer. Somehow, he was going to have to deal with his emotions, although it wasn't going to be easy after what had happened at the beach.

He groaned when the now-familiar pictures flooded into his head. He'd kept having flashbacks to that moment when he had held her in his arms all weekend long. It was sheer torture to remember her sweetly ardent response, but he couldn't allow it to influence him. Maybe she did still feel something for him, but he had to think about the damage he could cause and not give in to this desire he felt to have her back in his life.

Everyone was assembled in his office when he arrived. It was a multi-disciplinary meeting so the room was crowded. As well as his team, there was a dietician, a radiographer, plus a member of the hospital's physiotherapy staff present. Normally, he looked forward to these meetings. They fulfilled a valuable role by providing an overall view of each child's progress. However, as he took his seat, he decided to cut it short that day. The less time he spent around Kelly at the moment, the better.

'First on the agenda are Stefano and Sebastiano Bianchi,' he said, cutting short the usual preliminaries. 'Have they begun physiotherapy yet?'

He listened attentively as the physiotherapist explained that the boys were responding well to treatment. They had managed to shift a lot of the mucus that had formed in the small airways in their lungs and both boys were breathing much easier now.

Luca nodded. 'Good. I'll review the case again on Wednesday. If the boys have continued to make progress, they can be discharged then. Please make a note of that in their file, Dr Carlyon.'

He passed the file to Kelly for no other reason than she happened to be closest to his desk. Taking another set of notes off the pile, he stared blankly at the pages. Even though Kelly hadn't uttered a word, he was so aware of her at that moment that he seemed to have lost the ability to function properly. Pictures suddenly began to flash inside his head again, images of them locked in one another's arms, and he almost groaned out loud in frustration. How in heaven's name was he expected to do his job?

'Are those Ilaria's notes?' Carlo leant across the desk, mercifully breaking the spell.

Luca finally focused on the page and nodded. 'Yes. Have we had the results of those tests we ordered?'

'The results of the lumbar puncture came back late on Friday,' Kelly told him quietly. 'There were blast cells present in the cerebrospinal fluid.'

'Has a date been arranged for the bone-marrow biopsy?' he said curtly, because it was the only way he could keep a check on his emotions.

'We're waiting for it to come through,' she explained.

'Then get on to the oncology department and chase it up. We can't afford to be hanging around. This needs to be sorted out immediately.'

Once again he handed the file to her, only this time he made the mistake of looking at her. His heart ached when he saw the hurt in her eyes. He knew that he had been far too sharp with her but if he once gave in to the feelings whirling about inside him, he would never be able to hold out. He would tell her that he loved her and that was the last thing he must do.

The meeting came to an end at last. Luca had another clinic after it was over so he headed straight to the outpatients department. It was another long list but it was a relief to immerse himself in his patients' problems instead of his own. By the time the clinic finished it was lunchtime, but he decided against going to the canteen in case Kelly was there. He couldn't risk having his hard-won equilibrium shattered again that day.

He bought himself a cup of coffee from the café and went out into the garden. There were benches dotted around the grounds so he found himself a quiet spot and sat down. He had just taken his first sip of coffee when he heard footsteps coming along the path and, looking up, he saw Kelly coming towards him.

She stopped when she saw him sitting on the bench and he saw the colour drain from her face. He knew that she was going to turn tail and run and realised that he had to do something. They couldn't carry on avoiding each other when they had to work together.

'Please don't run away,' he said quickly, standing up.

'I…I don't want to intrude,' she said quietly.

'You're not.' He sighed when he saw her glance over her shoulder. 'Look, Kelly, I know how awkward you feel about what happened on Saturday because I feel the same way. But we have to get over it if we're going to work together.'

'Do you really think we can work together now?'

'I don't know, but I'm willing to give it another try if you are.' He took a deep breath but the words needed to be said. 'I care about you a great deal, and I don't want to hurt you. I know how important this job is to you and I would hate to think that you had to give it up because of me.'

'I don't want to give it up, but it might be the best thing to do,' she said, her voice catching. 'I don't want to hurt you either, Luca, but if I stay here there's no guarantee that we won't end up hurting each other, is there?'

'No, there isn't. All we can do is try to make the situation as easy as possible for ourselves.'

'That's what you said when you suggested we should try being friends,' she pointed out. 'It didn't work, though.'

'Then maybe we need to find another way. Maybe we were expecting too much of ourselves.'

'What do you mean?' she said slowly.

Luca felt his heart begin to pound. He could be making the biggest mistake of his life but what choice did he have? Kelly would quit her job unless he persuaded her they could resolve this issue.

'That friendship isn't enough for either of us, not for you and certainly not for me.' He took a step towards her, suddenly desperate to convince her that his plan could work. After all, it had worked once before and there was no reason why it wouldn't work again.

He captured her hands, feeling the shudder that ran through her. 'I want more than friendship from you, Kelly, and I think you feel the same way.'

'I don't know what you mean,' she said sharply.

'Yes, you do. You know exactly what I mean,' he said

softly, watching her face so that he saw the colour come flooding back. 'We were lovers as well as colleagues once before, and it worked then. There's no reason why it can't work for us again.'

CHAPTER THIRTEEN

KELLY felt the ground suddenly tilt and was glad that Luca had such a firm hold on her. When he led her to the bench and sat her down, she didn't protest for the simple reason that words were beyond her. Her head was whirling but through all the confusion one thought was crystal clear: Luca wanted them to be lovers.

'You can't mean that!' she exclaimed. 'It's the craziest idea I've ever heard.'

'Why is it crazy?' He leant forward and she shivered when she saw the light of conviction in his eyes. 'We were good together, Kelly, and you can't deny it.'

'I'm not denying it. But that was then and this is now, and an awful lot has happened in between,' she said harshly.

'I know that, *cara*.' He cupped her cheek in his hand and his gaze was so tender that it brought tears to her eyes. 'However, it doesn't alter the fact that I want to be with you.'

'Don't do this, Luca,' she pleaded, turning her head so that he was forced to remove his hand.

'And if I don't, what will happen? Will you stay on here or will the situation become so stressful that you will be forced to leave?' His tone was harsh. 'I don't want to see you ruin your career, Kelly, but that's what will happen if you break your contract. You know as well as I do how a future employer would view it if you upped and left a job like this without a very good reason. You need to demonstrate commitment if you intend to reach the top. You can't allow anything or anyone to stand in your way.'

'And to demonstrate my commitment I should have an affair with you? Is that what you're saying?' She laughed scornfully. 'I thought it was only in films that the casting-couch routine was used, but it just shows how naïve I am.'

'You know that isn't what I'm suggesting. I'm not asking you to sleep with me to improve your chances of promotion.'

'Not in so many words, but the outcome would be the same.'

She glared back at him, whipping up her anger because she was afraid that she would agree to his proposal otherwise. Having Luca back would help to heal some of the pain, but she had to remember that it would be only a temporary relief. Once she left Sardinia, that would be the end of their affair and she didn't think she could go through the heartbreak of losing him a second time.

'It's completely different and if you give yourself time to think, you will realise that.' He stood up abruptly, looking big and arrogant as he stared down at her. 'The reason we've been experiencing all these problems at work is because of how we feel. I want you, Kelly, and I know you want me, too. Remember that when you make your decision.'

'I've already made it,' she declared, jumping to her feet. 'I am not having an affair with you, Luca. Not now, not ever.'

She pushed past him and ran back up the path to the hospital. She went straight to the ladies' washroom and sluiced her face with cold water, but the fever she could feel raging inside her didn't abate.

Plucking a paper towel out of the dispenser, she dried her face then stared at her reflection in the mirror. Was it really such a crazy idea, or was Luca right? One of the hardest things about this situation was having to fight her feelings all the time, but if she no longer had to do that, she would be able to concentrate on her job.

She sighed because that was the plus side, of course. The down side would come later, after she left Sardinia. Luca had made it clear that it would be a temporary arrangement and not a permanent one. Maybe he was confident that he could work this attraction he felt for her out of his system, but she wasn't convinced it would work for her. She simply couldn't envisage a time when she would no longer want him.

Luca found himself constantly watching the clock as the afternoon wore on. Although Kelly had dismissed his idea about them having an affair, he was hoping that she would realise it was the answer to their problems. However, by the time four o'clock arrived, he was starting to lose any hope of her seeing sense.

He made his way to the ward for the afternoon round, feeling the jolt his heart gave when the first person he saw there was Kelly. She was talking to one of the nurses and he saw the colour run up her face when she spotted him coming into the ward.

Luca's mouth compressed as he made his way to the first patient's bed. He was bitterly aware that he might have made the situation worse and that was the last thing he'd intended. The thought that Kelly might decide to leave immediately was more than he could bear so it was an effort to concentrate when Sister handed him the case notes.

The patient was a twelve-year-old boy called Paolo Rossi who had been diagnosed with diabetes mellitus two months earlier. Although Paulo had responded well since he had been prescribed insulin, he'd had a viral infection that week which had caused him to vomit repeatedly. His insulin levels now needed adjusting, which was why he had been admitted.

Luca smiled at the boy. 'You understand why you're here, don't you, Paolo?'

'*Si.*' The boy sighed. 'You have to alter the amount of insulin I'm taking.'

'That's right. If you're ill and start vomiting, it upsets the balance between the amount of glucose your body produces and the amount of insulin you need to take. I know it's a nuisance but we need to adjust your insulin levels to make sure that you remain as healthy as possible.'

'I wish I didn't have this stupid illness,' Paolo muttered. 'None of my friends have to give themselves injections every day, *and* they can eat and do anything they want, too.'

'I understand how frustrating it must be for you, but so long as you monitor your glucose levels very carefully there's no reason why you should stop doing the things you enjoy,' Luca said soothingly as he checked the boy's chart. 'It looks as though everything is settling down again. If your glucose levels are all right in the morning, you can go home after lunch.'

The rest of the round passed without incident and Luca was able to leave on time for once. However, as he got into his car to drive home, he was very aware that Kelly still hadn't made any attempt to speak to him. He sighed as he started the engine. It looked as though she had rejected his idea and although he understood why, he still believed it could have worked. All he could do was hope that he hadn't precipitated her into making a hasty decision about her future at the hospital.

Kelly went straight back to her apartment after she finished work. She'd not had anything to eat that day yet the thought of making herself a meal was more than she could bear. What was she going to do about this idea of Luca's? Should she tell him it was out of the question or should she give it some thought? What if he was right and it would help?

She paced the sitting room in a fever of uncertainty. Whatever she decided, there would be repercussions and it was trying to work out which option would cause the least amount of problems that was so difficult. However, no matter how hard she tried to think it all through, it was impossible to make the decision on her own. She needed to speak to Luca and find out exactly what he was proposing before she made up her mind.

Snatching up her bag, she left the apartment. The sun was just dipping below the surrounding hills when she reached his villa. She paused for a moment while she mustered up her courage then rang the bell. Maria answered and ushered her into the sitting room before she went to find Luca.

Kelly walked over to the window. Her stomach was twisting itself into knots but she had to find out if Luca was right. One thing was certain: they couldn't carry on the way they had been doing. If she didn't accept his offer, she would have to leave, no matter what damage it would cause to her career.

'*Buona sera,* Kelly.'

All of a sudden Luca was there in the room with her and her heart went into overdrive when she saw him. For a moment she couldn't think of a word to say as panic engulfed her so it was left to him to take charge.

'Have you had dinner yet? Matteo and I were just about to eat when you rang the bell. Why don't you join us?'

'I…I don't want to get in the way,' she said haltingly.

'Of course you aren't in the way.' He smiled at her, his handsome face filled with so much warmth that some of her panic subsided. 'Matteo will be thrilled to see you. He's not stopped talking about you all weekend. Come along.'

He ushered her out of the room before she had time to think about what was happening. Opening a door on the opposite side of the hall, he led her out to the garden. Kelly stopped and looked around in delight. Tall, slender cypress trees provided a dramatic backdrop for the colourful flower-beds and emerald-green lawn as well as providing welcome areas of shade. There was even a swimming pool, surrounded by a wrought-iron fence to stop Matteo accidentally falling into the water. It was the most beautiful garden she had ever seen and she couldn't hide her pleasure as she turned to Luca.

'It's absolutely gorgeous. You must love living here.'

'I do. I never imagined I would own a house as beautiful as this. I feel extremely fortunate to live here.'

Kelly smiled, touched by the humility in his voice. 'It has nothing to do with luck, Luca,' she admonished gently. 'You've worked hard and earned all this. You deserve it.'

'Thank you.'

His eyes were gentle and her heart fluttered when she saw the expression they held. All of a sudden it felt as though they were back to where they'd been two years ago. They'd enjoyed the most wonderful rapport then—perhaps they could rediscover it.

The thought filled her with excitement. It was hard not to let Luca see how she felt as he led her to the patio where a table had been laid for dinner. Matteo squealed with delight when he saw her and Kelly laughed as she bent down to kiss him. 'What a lovely welcome.'

'Please, sit down.' Luca pulled out a chair for her then filled a glass with wine and set it beside her place. He was the perfect host yet she sensed that he was impatient to get the meal over so they could get down to the reason for her visit. Her hands shook as she helped herself to a piece of *su pani carasau*—wafer-thin sheets of bread made from flour and semolina—and dipped it into the bowls of olive oil and salt next to her plate because she still wasn't sure what she was going to do.

'I'm addicted to this bread,' she explained, striving to find a neutral topic of conversation. 'It tastes so delicious.'

Luca smiled. 'You're turning into a real Sardinian.'

'I doubt if I could pass for Sardinian with my hair colour.'

'Oh, I don't know. What about all those wonderful paintings by Titian? The models had the same glorious hair colour as you have.'

The appreciation in his voice sent a shiver scudding through her. There wasn't a doubt in her mind at that moment that Luca was deeply attracted to her. But he certainly hadn't said that he was in love with her and she must never let herself forget that if she embarked on this affair. She couldn't afford to let herself hope for something that was never going to happen.

Luca tried his best to keep his emotions in check but it wasn't easy. He still didn't know what Kelly was going to do and the strain was playing havoc with his self-control. He lifted Matteo out of his high-chair, trying his hardest to carry on as normal.

'You can play with your toys while we finish dinner,' he said, setting the little boy down on the grass. He watched as the child hurried over to his toys then sat down again, trying to control the rapid beating of his heart as he turned to Kelly. He needed to remain calm if he hoped to convince her that this plan could work. 'Would you like some coffee?'

'No, thank you. This is fine.' She took a sip of her wine then placed the glass carefully on the table. 'I've been trying to decide whether this idea of yours could work.'

'And what have you decided?' he asked as calmly as he could.

'I haven't.' She shrugged. 'It sounds so crazy. We have an affair in the hope that it will ease the problems we're experiencing at work.'

'It's not quite as clinical as that,' he said quietly. 'I don't want to have an affair with you just because of work, Kelly. There's more to it than that.'

'Is there?' She shrugged again, although he could tell that she was nowhere near as relaxed as she was pretending to be. 'That wasn't the impression I got earlier on today.'

'Probably not.' He sighed. 'I made a real mess of it, didn't I? No wonder you thought I was mad to suggest it.'

'So explain it to me again.' She leant forward and he could see the urgency in her eyes. 'I need to know exactly what I'm letting myself in for, Luca. I don't want to end up feeling the way I did when we spilt up before.'

'It's the last thing I want, too.' He captured her hand and held it tightly, overwhelmed with guilt when he heard the pain in her voice. 'I never meant to hurt you like that, Kelly.'

'I got over it. It's the present that matters now, what we're going to do about this problem we have.'

Her tone was clipped and that made him feel even worse. Despite her assertions to the contrary, he knew that his betrayal still hurt her. All he could do was to try and make this situation as easy as possible for her.

'You're right. We need to concentrate on the present,' he said with a firmness he wished he felt. 'My biggest concern is that what's been happening recently could adversely affect your career. You are a first-rate doctor, Kelly, and you will go far so long as you remain focused.'

'Which I've been finding extremely difficult to do lately.' She looked steadily back at him. 'I'll admit that I find it hard to be around you, Luca. I did hope it would help if we tried being friends, but it wasn't enough, was it? We're still attracted to one another and maybe you're right to suggest that we should get it out of our systems so we can both move on.'

That hadn't been exactly what he had said but he wasn't in a position to correct her. 'I'm glad you realise that it could work.'

'I think it could so long as we both understand the rules.'

'And they are?'

'That we make sure nobody finds out about us. I don't want to find myself the subject of any gossip. That would be almost as damaging as if I left without working out my contract.' She paused then carried on. 'I also want to make it clear that when I leave here that will be the end. It will be easier for both of us if we accept that there is a time limit on our relationship, don't you think?'

He nodded, not trusting himself to speak in case he gave himself away. He didn't want to spend a few paltry months with her; he wanted a whole lifetime to love and cherish her. It was hard to contain his anguish as she continued.

'My contract was for six months, with the option to extend it if I wanted to do so. I had intended to stay here for a year at least, but I don't think that would be a good idea now.' She shrugged. 'Even if we've managed to work each other out of our systems by then, I think it would be better if I found myself another post.'

'If that's what you want then I'm happy to go along with it,' he said tightly. He cleared his throat when he saw the look she shot him. Maybe the thought of losing her in a few months' time was ripping his heart to shreds but that was his problem and he had to deal with it. If he could stop her making a decision that would impact badly on her career, it would be worth all the heartache.

'I'll keep my eyes open for anything suitable for you. I have a number of contacts and I would be happy to recommend you if a job came up.'

'Thank you, but I don't want any favours. If I'm to make it to the top, I shall do it on my own.'

'Fine.' He knew she was right because it was how he had always felt, but it still hurt to have her reject his help. 'You know what you're doing.'

'I do. It took me a long time to get my life back on track after we split up and I don't intend to make any more mistakes. My work means everything to me, far more than anything else will ever do.'

If that had been a reminder about where he featured in her life, it had struck home. Luca stood up abruptly, afraid that he would make the mistake of letting her see how difficult he found it to behave so coldly. It was as though she had set aside all her emotions and was viewing his proposal as a business proposition, and that was something he hadn't anticipated.

'It's time Matteo had his bath. I'll take him in while you finish your wine.'

He turned to go then stopped when she said softly, 'Do you want me to leave after that?'

Luca felt his heart start to pound. He knew that if she stayed the night, there would be no going back. They would be committed to this affair for however long it took her to get him out of her system. Could he handle that? Could he face the thought of waking up each morning, wondering if today would be the day when she no longer needed him?

He knew how devastated he was going to feel when it happened, but she needed to work out her contract at the hospital. And if that meant him living on a knife edge, that was what he had to do. He turned to her, almost overwhelmed by sadness.

'I'd like you to stay, Kelly. If you want to.'

CHAPTER FOURTEEN

THE light had faded now but Kelly stayed where she was. Oddly enough, she no longer felt confused. Now the decision had been made, she felt much calmer, although how she would feel in the morning was another matter.

Her mind shied away from the thought of what the morning might bring as she stood up and walked to the pool. Opening the gate in the fence, she bent down and trailed her fingers in the water. The pool lights had come on as soon as it had grown dark and the water gleamed an iridescent sapphire blue. It looked wonderfully inviting.

'There's some spare swimsuits in the house if you fancy a swim.'

She glanced round when Luca appeared, feeling her heart leap as she watched him walk towards her. She had always found him incredibly attractive and that hadn't changed. It was just the circumstances that were different now. This wasn't going to be the lifetime's commitment she had dreamed of, but a brief affair. And when it was over she would move on.

She stood up, refusing to acknowledge the tiny voice inside her head that was telling her that she would never stop loving him. She had made her decision and she was going to abide by it.

'It sounds good to me, but how about you? Are you coming in as well?'

'Why not? It's not often I have an excuse to do nothing all evening.'

'Don't tell me you usually work when you get home from the hospital?' she exclaimed as she followed him into the villa.

'I'm afraid so.' He grimaced. 'I usually retreat to my study once Matteo is in bed and try to catch up with all the paperwork I didn't have time to do during the day. I can access my office computer from here which makes life a lot easier.'

'But you shouldn't spend your evenings working,' she protested. 'You need to take some time for yourself to recharge your batteries.'

'Nobody forces me to do it,' he said lightly, opening the door to the elegantly appointed cloakroom. 'I just find it easier to do the paperwork at home so that I can devote my time at work to seeing patients.'

He opened a cupboard and showed her where the swimsuits were kept, effectively bringing the discussion to an end. Kelly sorted through the selection after he left and chose a plain red suit similar in style to her own swimsuit. She quickly undressed and put it on, thinking about what he had told her.

It seemed wrong that Luca should spend so much time working. It appeared that his only periods of relaxation came when he was caring for Matteo and it didn't seem right that his life should be so restricted. The thought nagged away at her as she pulled on a towelling robe and made her way out to the garden. Luca was already in the pool when she got there, swimming up and down in an efficiently elegant crawl. Kelly paused on the side so she could watch him. He reached the end of the pool and turned, and she felt her breath catch when he saw her. His gaze skimmed over her and she felt a rush of heat invade her. It was all she could do not to turn tail when he swam over to her.

'Are you coming in, or are you going to stand there all night?' he asked with a grin that didn't quite conceal the hunger in his eyes.

'I'm trying to decide if the water is warm enough.' She daintily dipped her toes into the water as though she was testing its temperature. If she was to get through the next few months unscathed then she needed to hold part of herself back. She simply couldn't afford to let him know the effect he had on her. 'Hmm, it feels rather cold to me.'

'Cold?' he echoed. 'It's not cold at all, it's perfect. Feel.' Scooping up a handful of water, he let it dribble down her bare legs. 'Now, does that feel cold?'

'Yes, it does. It's freezing.' She glared at him then gasped when he caught hold of her hand and tugged on it. 'No. Stop it. You mustn't... Luca!'

His name erupted from her lips as she suddenly found herself tumbling into the water. She managed to take a deep breath before she submerged and came up spluttering, with outrage as much as shock. 'I can't believe you just did that.'

'Me neither.' His smile widened as he tucked a long wet strand of hair behind her ear. 'Normally I abhor that kind of irresponsible behaviour. Obviously, you have a very bad effect on me, Dr Carlyon.'

Kelly shivered when she felt his fingers brush her skin

again. She could feel ripples of sensation spreading from the spot where his hand had touched and bit her lip. She had to hold back and not throw herself, heart and soul, into this affair. Tossing back her hair, she plunged beneath the surface of the water. Although she knew there would be more moments like that to come, she wanted them to happen on her terms. She intended to be fully in control of herself when they made love.

The thought sent a wave of heat racing through her as she set off down the pool. She swam faster than normal and was already tiring before she reached the side. When Luca suddenly appeared beside her, she missed her stroke and would have sunk if he hadn't grabbed hold of her.

'Don't do that,' she said, glaring at him as she trod water.

'Sorry. I assumed we were having a race when you set off like a torpedo.'

'I just thought I'd get some exercise,' she muttered, knowing how lame that sounded.

He sighed softly. 'It's OK to feel scared, Kelly. This is a whole new experience for both of us, and I feel as keyed up as you do.'

She bit her lip when she heard the tenderness in his voice. 'Do you?'

'Yes.' He put his arms around her and drew her to him. 'I feel as though I'm on some kind of emotional roller-coaster. My insides are all churned up and I'm having difficulty thinking. I'm not sure what to do about it, but maybe this will help…'

He didn't finish the sentence because his mouth had already found hers by that point. Kelly felt a jolt of electricity arc through her as his lips claimed hers in a searing kiss that said more than he probably realised about his feelings for her. Maybe Luca had suggested this affair as a means to an end, but that didn't alter the fact that he wanted her.

The thought unlocked her own passion and she kissed him back with a hunger she couldn't hide. His lips were hard and demanding but she was more than willing to give him what he wanted as well as take what she needed, too. They clung to each other for a long moment before they broke apart, and she could see the fire that burned in his eyes and knew that he could see the same heat in hers.

'I want you so much, *cara mia*,' he murmured.

'I want you, too,' she admitted, shuddering when he drew her to him again so that she could feel the hardness of his arousal pressing against her.

He kissed her again and she closed her eyes while she savoured the sensations that were flowing through her. The water lapped over their heads as they sank to the bottom of the pool, their bodies entwined, their mouths still fused. When they floated back to the surface, Luca took her face between his hands and looked deep into her eyes.

'I need to be sure this is what you really want, Kelly. If you have any doubts about what we're doing, say so now. I couldn't bear it if I hurt you again.'

Her eyes filled with tears when she heard the anguish in his voice. There wasn't a doubt in her mind that he was telling her the truth and something warm and tender blossomed inside her, making a mockery of her plans to hold part of herself back. She realised then that, no matter how long their affair lasted, she would give him her heart.

'I'm sure. It's what I want, Luca. It's what I need, too.'

He closed his eyes as though he was memorising the words

then kissed her again, setting a seal on their new relationship. Kelly clung to him as he trailed kisses over her face and down her neck. Everywhere his mouth touched, her skin burned, liquid fire spreading through every cell until she was consumed by heat. When he slid his fingers under the straps of her swimsuit and drew them down her arms, she was trembling with need, but so was he.

'You're so beautiful,' he said reverently as he studied her bare breasts. 'So very, very beautiful.'

His head dipped and she cried out in pleasure when she felt his mouth close over her wet nipple as he suckled her. He lavished the same attention on her other breast then stripped off her swimsuit. His swimming trunks swiftly followed and then they were both naked, both hungry and both eager for one another's bodies.

He swam with her to where the water was a little shallower then lifted her in his arms. Kelly gasped when she felt him glide inside her with an ease that proved how much they wanted one another. They made love right there in the pool and it was the most intense experience of her life, the coolness of the water lapping around her, providing an erotic contrast to the heat of him inside her.

Luca cradled her in his arms when it was over and she could feel the deep shudders of fulfilment which rocked him. 'I never thought I could feel like this again,' he whispered against her throat.

'It was perfect, wasn't it?' she said, unable to pretend that it had meant nothing to her.

'It was. Just like you, Kelly. Perfect in every way.' He kissed her softly on the mouth then helped her out of the pool, picking up the robe she'd discarded and wrapping it around her with a tender concern that touched her. Maybe he didn't love her but he cared about her, and that was something to remember.

He wrapped a towel round his waist then scooped their swimsuits out of the water. 'We'd better not leave any evidence of what we've been up to,' he said, smiling as he draped the wet swimsuits over the end of a sun bed.

Kelly blushed. 'Maria would be shocked if she found them there in the morning.'

'I wasn't thinking about Maria. Young as he is, I had visions of Matteo finding them and all the questions he would ask.' He sighed as he lifted her hand to his lips and kissed her palm. 'I need more time to prepare myself before I have to give him the "birds and the bees" talk.'

Kelly laughed out loud. 'Don't tell me you'll be embarrassed when the time comes, Luca? And you a doctor, too.'

'Oh, I should be able to manage it if I stick to the facts.' He swung her round so that they were standing hip to hip. 'However, a factual discourse on the mechanics of human reproduction is somewhat different to answering the questions of a curious two-year-old who wants to know why his daddy and his friend have left their swimsuits in the pool. I could find myself somewhat stuck for words then.'

Kelly chuckled, enjoying the fact that he could poke fun at himself. 'I'm sure you would make a brilliant job of it if you had to.'

'Thank you. I'm touched by your faith in me.' He rewarded her with a kiss then linked his fingers through hers and led her up the path to the villa. 'There's towels and a hairdryer in the cloakroom if you want to take a shower. I'll put some coffee on while you're doing that.'

'Great. I could do with a cup to get rid of the taste of that chlorine.' She grinned at him. 'I seem to have swallowed rather a lot of water.'

'Sorry.' He kissed her again and his expression was wry. 'I didn't actually plan what happened just now, not that it's any excuse.'

'You don't need an excuse.' Reaching up she kissed him on the mouth. 'I wanted it as much as you did.'

His eyes darkened as he pulled her back into his arms. 'I just hope it helps, Kelly. I don't want you to feel that you have to leave because of me.'

He kissed her again and she shivered when she felt the desperation in the kiss as well as the desire. Why was he so determined to safeguard her career? she wondered, but it was impossible to work out the answer while he was kissing her. When he lifted her into his arms and carried her along the hall to his bedroom, she didn't protest. She wanted him, too, wanted to experience the passion and the fulfilment that he could give her because it was the only way she could feel truly whole. When she was in his arms, in his bed, when he was inside her, she no longer felt alone or scared about the future. All that mattered was the moment, the experience of loving Luca and being close to him.

He laid her down in the centre of his bed then switched on the lamps. All she had on was the robe and it took only seconds to dispense with it. Luca dropped the towel he was wearing onto the floor and lay down beside her so that she could feel his body pulsing against her and proclaiming his hunger for her.

'I don't think I will ever get tired of looking at you, Kelly,' he said as he gazed at her. 'I'll never get tired of touching you either.'

His hand skimmed down her throat and over her breasts, tracing the dip of her waist and the fullness of her hips before it came to rest at the junction of her thighs. Kelly pressed her lips tightly together in case she cried out when she felt him start to stroke her. She could feel herself growing hot and damp but he resisted when she tried to encourage him to make love to her. Bending, he ran the tip of his tongue over her left nipple until it peaked then repeated the process with her right breast, and all the time his clever, tormenting fingers were working their magic on her.

She gasped when she felt the first spasm grip her. 'Luca, please,' she whispered, her eyes closing as she fought to contain the feelings that were building inside her.

'Look at me, Kelly. I want to see when it happens to you, *cara.*'

His voice seemed to be coming from a long way off, but she managed to obey the instruction and opened her eyes for him. His fingers stroked her again and another spasm rocked her and then another until the world suddenly dissolved into a shower of stars and light. And all the time it was happening, Luca was watching her, sharing the experience with her as well as creating it.

'Now it's your turn,' he whispered, pressing a kiss to her lips.

Kelly wasn't sure what he meant at first. Her mind was still awash with all the sensations that were flowing through her. She gasped when he rolled over onto his back and lifted her so that she could straddle him. Holding her gaze, he gently eased her down until he was sheathed inside her. Kelly gripped hold of his shoulders as he started moving, slowly at first then faster. And all the time he was watching her and she was watching him.

Shock coursed through when she saw the exact moment he lost control as passion claimed him. That he had allowed her to see him at his most vulnerable almost reduced her to tears but before they could fall, she felt her own passion building once more.

Luca cushioned her against his chest as she climaxed for a second time, and held her long after it was over, stroking her hair and murmuring to her. He seemed in no hurry to let her go and it was that which touched her more than anything else, the fact that he needed this closeness as much as she did. As she drifted off to sleep, she found herself praying that he might learn how to love her again one day. It could take a long time but she was willing to wait. And if it did happen then she would tell him the truth—that she loved him and had never stopped loving him despite what had happened.

Maybe, just maybe, her dreams would come true one day.

CHAPTER FIFTEEN

THAT night was the first of many and Kelly spent almost every night with Luca after that. They were extremely discreet, though, and made sure that nobody found out about their affair. Luca treated her no differently than any other member of his team when they were in work. The only change was that they got along much better now. There was less friction between them and she soon found her confidence coming back.

Although the situation had improved dramatically, there were some problems that hadn't been resolved. Letizia continued to be extremely hostile towards her and never missed an opportunity to put her down. The situation grew even worse once it was announced that applications would soon be sought for the new senior registrar's post. Letizia was desperate to get the job and equally determined that Kelly would be out of the running. Although Kelly tried explaining that she would be leaving at the end of her contract and wouldn't be applying for the post, Letizia didn't believe her.

In the end, Kelly had to accept that she'd done everything she could and ignored the spiteful comments. She was determined to make the most of her time at the hospital and didn't intend to allow anyone to spoil it for her. If she couldn't have Luca, at least she would have her work, and a good reference from the Santa Margherita Ospedale would pave the way towards success in her chosen field.

It was on a Thursday evening, three weeks after she'd spent that first night with Luca, that things came to a head. She was about to leave work when Paolo Rossi was rushed into hospital, having suffered a hypoglycaemic attack. The staff in Pronto Soccorso administered an injection of glucose solution to counteract the lack of glucose in his blood and then transferred him to the ward. Kelly went to meet him as the porters wheeled him in.

'Hi, Paolo. How do you feel?'

'A bit better,' Paolo muttered, drowsily.

'We'll get you into bed and then see how you're doing,' she assured him.

She got him settled then sat down beside the bed. Paolo's parents hadn't arrived yet but she decided not to wait for them. It was vital that she establish what had gone wrong as quickly as possible.

'Right, Paolo, I need to find out why this has happened. Are you sure you injected the correct amount of insulin this morning?'

'Yes. My mum always checks to make sure I've got it right. She treats me like a baby,' the boy added in disgust.

Kelly smiled. 'It's only because she's worried about you, Paolo. Once she gets used to the situation she will feel a lot more confident about you handling things on your own.'

'I wish.' Paolo's sigh said everything that needed to be said about that theory so Kelly swiftly moved on. She didn't want to alienate him before she'd got to the root of the problem.

'So we've established that you injected yourself with the correct amount of insulin this morning. That means you must either have missed a meal, not eaten sufficient carbohydrates or done too much exercise. Have you any idea which it could be, Paolo?'

'Why should it have been any of those things?' the boy protested. 'It could just have happened.'

'That's highly unlikely,' Kelly said firmly. 'You had a hypoglycaemic attack, Paolo, which is caused by an abnormally low level of glucose in your blood. You understand the mechanics of having diabetes, don't you? Your doctor did explain it to you when you were diagnosed?'

Paolo shrugged. 'He said something about my pancreas not working properly. I didn't really understand what he meant.'

Kelly sighed. She was a firm believer in telling a child exactly what was going on so that he understood why he needed to take his medication. However, it seemed that Paolo's doctor had been less than forthcoming on the subject.

'It might help if I explain it to you again, then. Normally, the pancreas produces a hormone called insulin that regulates the level of glucose in the blood. In your case, though, insufficient insulin is being produced, which is why you need to have those injections every morning.'

'So this insulin I inject is only what my body should have made?' Paulo said, sounding a little more interested.

'That's right. It isn't medicine as such. It's something your body needs to function properly. So as long as you get the correct balance between the amount of food you eat and the amount of insulin you inject, you shouldn't have a problem. However, if you miss a meal or inject too much insulin, things will start to go wrong.'

She waited for a moment to make sure he had understood then carried on. 'Did you eat your lunch today, Paolo?'

'No,' he admitted. 'I threw my sandwiches away. My friends had organised a game of football during our lunch-break, you see, and I didn't have time to eat them.'

'Did you have anything at all to eat?' Kelly probed gently because now wasn't the time to berate him for being so foolish.

'An apple,' he muttered, avoiding her eyes.

'I see. Well, at least we've solved the mystery of why this attack happened. You skipped your lunch and played football. It meant there was far too much insulin in your body and not enough food to balance it. That's why you felt so dizzy and were complaining of double vision.'

'My friends thought I was drunk,' Paolo said, grinning. 'I was staggering about all over the place.'

'People in the throes of a hypoglycaemic attack are often wrongly thought to be under the influence of alcohol. The symptoms can be very similar, loss of co-ordination and sometimes quite aggressive behaviour. It's all because the brain is being starved of sufficient glucose to keep it func-tioning properly.'

'It was quite scary,' the boy admitted. 'I felt really odd and I didn't know why. I wish the other doctor had explained it to me like you just did. I would never have thrown away my sandwiches.'

'The most important thing is that you won't do it again, will you?' Kelly smiled when he shook his head. 'Good. I know it must be a nuisance having to give yourself those injections and watch what you eat, but it's the only way of keeping your diabetes under control. If you do exactly what you're told then you'll be able to join in and do everything your friends can do.'

'Do you mean that? It's not just something grown-ups say to make us kids feel better?'

'It's the truth, Paolo. Cross my heart and hope to die.'

She made a cross over her heart, earning herself a little chuckle. She checked his obs again and noted them down on the sheet then signed it. There was no need to alter his insulin intake so she didn't make any adjustment to the dosage. Now that she knew the reason for this attack, the problem would right itself.

She left the hospital a short time later and went straight to her apartment to get changed. Luca was expecting her for dinner and she wanted to be sure that she looked her best. The cotton sundress she put on had been an impulse buy in the sales. There'd been little opportunity to wear it in rainy Manchester but it was perfect for this Mediterranean paradise. Made from soft yellow cotton, it made the most of her slender figure and stunning red hair.

When she left the apartment a short time later, she found it difficult to contain her excitement. She knew that Luca would appreciate the trouble she'd gone to and it sent a buzz of heat through her veins to imagine what would happen later that night. No matter how many times they made love, it was always the most magical of experiences. When she was in Luca's arms, she could almost believe that they would be together for ever.

Luca was late getting home. He'd had a meeting with the management team to finalise the wording of the advertisement for the new senior registrar's post. The job was being advertised in all the major journals so it looked as though he would have his pick of candidates. As he swung the car in through the gates of the villa, however, he couldn't help wishing that he could simply offer the post to Kelly. She seemed to have regained her confidence in the past few weeks and there had been no more slip-ups. He wouldn't find anyone better than her, but offering her the job would mean her having to stay on here. Even though these past three weeks had been the most wonderful of his entire life, he knew that it had to end. It wouldn't be fair to Kelly to tie her to him if it meant she would miss out on other opportunities in the future.

The thought hung heavily over him as he entered the villa. Matteo came running to meet him, jabbering away nineteen to the dozen as he told him about his day. Luca lifted him up and swung him round, drawing comfort from the child's laughter. He couldn't have Kelly but he would devote his life to making sure Matteo was safe and happy. And when Matteo grew up and no longer needed him, at least he would have the consolation of knowing that he had done his very best for him.

He carried the little boy into the kitchen and stood him on a stool. Maria was having a rare evening off and as soon as she left, he and Matteo set about making dinner. They were just about to put the pasta in the pan when the bell rang.

'Kelly!' Matteo scrambled down off his stool and raced to the door, bouncing up and down in a fever of impatience as he waited for Luca to open it.

Luca undid the lock, feeling his heart leap when he saw Kelly. She looked so beautiful that it was all he could do not to sweep her into his arms right there and then. He kissed her chastely on the cheek, mindful of his son's sharp-eyed gaze. They had managed to avoid any awkward questions so far because Kelly made a point of leaving before Matteo woke up. Nevertheless, it was hard to restrain himself when what he wanted most of all was to kiss her until they were both dizzy.

'You look lovely,' he said as he closed the door. 'I like your dress.'

'Thank you. I chose it especially.'

Her green eyes filled with warmth as she smiled at him and he felt his insides lurch. It took a massive effort of will to keep his hands at his sides as he ushered her into the kitchen. Matteo skipped along beside them, chattering away in an odd mixture of Italian and English. The little boy had picked up a lot of English words from listening to him and Kelly talking, although his rather unique blending of the two languages sometimes caused them to smile.

Luca smiled as he listened to them. They had a real rapport and it pleased him to see how Matteo had blossomed. It wasn't only his life that had been made so much better by having Kelly share it, but his son's as well.

The thought caused him some disquiet. He knew that Matteo was going to miss her when she left Sardinia. However, he consoled himself with the thought that children were extremely adaptable so it shouldn't cause Matteo any lasting damage.

Once the pasta was ready, Luca tipped it onto a serving dish and placed it on the table. There was a simple tomato sauce to go with it, redolent with herbs and garlic; Kelly sniffed appreciatively when he placed the bowl on the table.

'That smells absolutely wonderful. I'm starving.'

'Then sit yourself down and tuck in.' Luca smiled as he heaped her plate with malloreddus—the small, grooved, saffron-flavoured pasta which was a speciality of the island—then handed her a dish of freshly grated local cheese. 'Try some of this with it. It's similar to Parmesan and I think you'll like it.'

She sprinkled some over her pasta and tucked in. 'Mmm, it's gorgeous. What is it?'

'Pecorino romano.' He lifted Matteo into his high-chair and sat down. 'It's made from sheep's milk that has been boiled first. It has quite a strong flavour and can be a bit too pungent for some people's taste, but it's a favourite of mine.'

'It's really delicious and so is the sauce.' She waved her fork at him. 'My compliments to the chef.'

'Make that chefs,' Luca corrected. 'This little guy helped by washing all the herbs.'

'Really? Did you help your papa make dinner?' she said, turning to Matteo. She smiled when the little boy solemnly nodded. 'Well, I think you are a very clever boy. It's delicious.'

Leaning across the table, she kissed Matteo on his cheek. Luca looked away, terrified that she would see how much the gesture had moved him. She obviously cared about Matteo and he sensed that she cared about him, too. If it weren't for her career, he would have moved heaven and earth to keep her here, but he couldn't risk ruining everything she had worked so hard to achieve.

It was a dispiriting thought and Luca found it hard to shake it off. After dinner was over, they played in the garden with Matteo until it was time for the little boy to go to bed. Luca gave him a bath and read a story to him then went back to the kitchen and found Kelly in the process of making them some coffee.

'You must have read my mind,' he said, slumping tiredly into a chair. 'I definitely need a shot of caffeine.'

'All that racing around taken it out of you, has it?' she teased as she placed the cups on the table.

Luca grasped her round the waist and pulled her down onto his lap. 'Oh, I think I can summon up enough energy to put you in your place, young lady,' he growled threateningly.

He kissed her long and hungrily, delighting in her unbridled response. When he lifted her into his arms and carried her to his bedroom, she clung to him. She was just as hungry for him as he was for her and the thought helped to ease some of the despair he felt.

They made love with a passion which shook him to the very core of his being. It didn't seem to matter that they'd made love the previous night because it felt as though they were starving for one another. As he entered her, Luca knew that nothing he did in his life could be better than this. Loving Kelly was the very pinnacle of all he had achieved; it was everything he had ever wanted. Surely there was a way to work through the problems. If she needed time and space to devote to her career, he would give it to her willingly if it meant she would come back to him. He would do anything it took, make any compromise demanded of him, but would it be enough? How did she feel? Was she willing to risk her career to spend her life with him?

It was a question he couldn't answer. It was also one he was afraid to ask because of the damage it could cause. He knew that she would find it difficult to refuse if he asked her to stay, but he didn't want her to make a life-changing decision based on emotion. She needed to think about it, calmly and rationally, but was it possible to do that, to choose between what your heart wanted and what your head knew was right?

He drew her to him, held her close, listened to the sound of her breathing as she drifted off to sleep, and knew he couldn't ask that of her. It was too much to expect and she had too much to lose if she made the wrong choice, particularly as he'd already let her down once. He couldn't bear to think that one day she might regret choosing him.

CHAPTER SIXTEEN

IT WAS late when Kelly woke up the following morning and she had to rush around, getting ready. Luca just had time to see her out before they heard Matteo calling so there was no time for any lingering goodbyes. One quick kiss and she was hurrying down the path.

There was a lot more traffic on the road than there normally was as she made her way to the hospital. It was almost time for the day shift to come on duty and there were a lot of members of staff arriving for work. Kelly kept her head down, hoping that nobody would notice her and wonder where she'd been. The last thing she wanted was for there to be any gossip about her and Luca so it was a relief when she reached her apartment without encountering anyone she knew.

She hurriedly changed then made her way to the ward, stopping dead when she saw the group of people clustered around Paolo Rossi's bed. Luca was there, too, and her heart sank when she saw him. It had to be really serious if he'd been summoned.

'What's happened?' she demanded as she hurried to the bed.

'An overdose of insulin.' Luca's tone was clipped as he drew up an injection of glucagon. He swabbed the boy's leg and smoothly injected it.

'An overdose?' Kelly repeated in horror. 'But how did it happen?'

'That is something we need to determine. However, it would appear from his notes that his usual dosage has been doubled.'

Luca didn't look at her as he bent over the boy again and Kelly felt a shiver run down her spine. It was obvious that he blamed her for the mistake, but she hadn't increased the dosage of insulin. Paolo should have received the same amount as normal—the amount she had written in his notes the previous night—so how could such a mistake have happened?

Thankfully, it wasn't long before Paolo recovered consciousness. He was very groggy, though, and Kelly knew he would need time to recover. She desperately wanted to do something to help, but she could tell from the attitude of the nursing staff that they thought she was to blame. When Luca curtly told her to go to his office and wait for him, she didn't protest. There was no point trying to explain that she hadn't done anything wrong. Once he had read the notes she'd made last night, he would realise that himself.

Kelly clung to that thought as she made her way to his office. She sat down on a chair, hoping it wouldn't be long before he came. She wanted to clear this up as quickly as possible and as soon as he appeared, she leapt to her feet.

'How is Paolo?'

'He will recover.' Luca's face was set as he closed the door. He waved her back to the chair then placed Paolo's notes on the desk and pointed to the top sheet. 'Is this your signature?'

Kelly barely glanced at it. 'Of course it is.'

'So you don't deny that you wrote down that instruction?'

'No. Why should I? Look, Luca, I don't know what you're implying—'

'I am not implying anything. I am stating a fact. As a result of your carelessness, Dr Carlyon, a child almost died.'

'My carelessness? But what happened had nothing to do with me,' she protested, stunned by the accusation.

'You have just confirmed that you wrote this instruction.' His voice echoed with anger as he stabbed a finger on the sheet. 'That makes you culpable, Dr Carlyon—*you* and nobody else.'

Kelly stared at the sheet of paper. It *was* her signature but she hadn't made any alteration to the amount of insulin the boy should have received so what did Luca mean? She gasped when her eyes focused on the figure written in the drugs column. It was almost double the amount that Paolo should have been given.

'But I didn't write that. I didn't alter the dosage and I most certainly didn't write an instruction to the effect that it should be almost double what he's been taking up till now.'

'Then explain how that figure has appeared in his file. Has it somehow magically written itself? Come along, Dr Carlyon, if you didn't write it, how did it get there?'

'I don't know. All I know is that I didn't put it there.' She leant forward, desperate to convince him. 'I *never* altered the amount of insulin Paolo was to receive.'

'Maybe you didn't do it deliberately but the outcome was the same.' He stood up and she felt her heart shrivel up when she saw the contempt in his eyes. 'You made a mistake that could have cost a child his life. It wasn't your first mistake either, Dr Carlyon. In the circumstances, I have no choice except to suspend you.'

'Suspend me? You're saying that you don't want me to work here any more?'

'That is correct. You can continue to use the staff accommodation while we carry out an investigation into this incident. However, you are to hand in your pass and any other hospital property you have in your possession.'

Kelly stood up as well, gripping tight hold of the chair as the room started to spin. 'You can't possibly believe I would make a mistake like this, Luca.'

'It isn't for me to judge. I shall leave that to the proper authorities. They will deal with the situation from here on.'

He strode to the door then paused and she winced when she saw the pain in his eyes. It proved beyond any doubt that he did believe she was to blame. 'I'm sorry, Kelly, but it's out of my hands now. I can't help you.'

Kelly sank back down onto the chair after he left and put her head in her hands. She knew that she wasn't responsible for what had happened, but she had no way of proving it, seeing as it was her signature on the notes. Had someone altered the dosage and left her to take the blame? But who would do such a thing?

Her head whirled as she struggled to make sense of it all. If only Luca had believed her then she knew they could have sorted out this mess together, but he'd made it clear that he held her responsible. It hurt unbearably to know how little faith he had in her but she couldn't afford to dwell on that thought at the moment. She needed to clear her name and to do that she had to find out who had altered the instructions on Paolo's file.

She left the office and went back to the ward, but before she could enter, Sister appeared. 'I'm sorry, Dr Carlyon, but I've had orders not to admit you.'

'Orders? What do you mean?' Kelly demanded.

'Dr Ferrero told me that you have been suspended,' the woman explained uncomfortably. 'Unfortunately, I cannot allow you access to the patients.'

'I see. In that case, I won't embarrass you any further, Sister.'

Kelly made her way back along the corridor to the office. There was nobody in there so she helped herself to an envelope and put her security pass in it. She wrote Luca's name on the front then left it on the blotter along with her stethoscope and pen torch. Carlo appeared as she was about to leave and she could tell how upset he was.

'I heard what happened, Kelly. Is there anything I can do to help?'

'Find out who altered that instruction in Paolo Rossi's file because I certainly didn't double the dosage of insulin he was supposed to receive.'

'You think someone deliberately changed it?' Carlo exclaimed.

'How else could it have happened?' She sighed. 'I know it sounds incredible, Carlo, but I didn't write that instruction. I *know* I didn't. So if I didn't do it, it means that someone else changed those figures. It wouldn't have been that difficult. All they needed to do was slip another digit in front of the figure I'd written and—hey, presto—there you have it.'

'But who would do such a thing? I mean, if Letizia hadn't been so quick to notice there was something wrong with the boy, he could have died.'

'Letizia? Are you saying that she was the one who realised there was something wrong with Paolo?' Kelly exclaimed.

'*Si.*' Carlo shrugged. 'She just happened to come in early this morning and noticed that Paolo was extremely agitated. She immediately raised the alarm and summoned Luca as well.'

'Did she indeed? And what reason did she give for turning up so early today?'

Carlo frowned. 'She mentioned something about needing to go through some case notes before clinic started. Why? Surely you don't think Letizia had anything to do with this?'

'I don't know. All I know is that I wrote down the correct dose of insulin last night and by this morning it had been changed.' Kelly knew she couldn't accuse the other woman of altering the notes when she had no proof. However, she was convinced that Letizia was behind it.

'It's easy to make a mistake, Kelly,' Carlo said gently, obviously loath to believe that anyone would deliberately place a patient at risk.

'I know that, and if I thought I'd made a mistake, I would own up. But I'm certain this wasn't my fault, Carlo.'

Carlo didn't say anything. Kelly sighed when she saw how troubled he looked. 'I'm sorry, Carlo. It's not fair to expect you to take my side. I shall have to prove that I'm innocent, although I'm not sure how I'm going to do it.'

'Let's hope the inquiry will resolve the issue,' Carlo said, obviously relieved to be let off the hook. 'Once the panel has considered all the facts, I'm sure they will reach the right conclusion.'

Kelly wished she had his faith in the system but she was very much afraid that the inquiry wouldn't find in her favour. She didn't say so, however; she just said goodbye and left. It took just a few minutes to walk back to her apartment but it felt like the longest walk of her life. She knew that it wouldn't be long before the whole hospital heard about her suspension, and the thought of everyone talking about her was extremely hard to bear. What made it worse was that Luca believed she was guilty. If he'd had any real feelings for her, he would have known she was innocent and not needed to have it proved to him.

That thought, coming on top of what had happened, was too much. Kelly flung herself down on her bed and wept. It looked as though she was about to lose both the man she loved and her precious career.

Luca found it difficult to believe what had happened. That Kelly should have made such a mistake would have been bad enough, but the fact that she had denied it was even worse. If only she had trusted him and owned up then he would have done everything he could to help her, but now he was power-less to intervene. It would be up to the inquiry committee to decide what action should be taken and he knew that they would come down very hard on her if they decided she was at fault.

A cloud of despair hung over him for the remainder of the day. By the time he left work that night, he found it hard to raise a smile when his secretary bade him goodnight. He took the lift down to the ground floor, wondering what he should do. Although he'd had no choice but suspend Kelly, he needed to see her. If she was prepared to admit that she had made a mistake, it might go in her favour. He couldn't bear to think that her whole career could be ruined because of this error.

He left the hospital and made his way to the staff quarters, uncaring if anyone saw him. This was far too important to worry about people gossiping. Kelly's apartment was on the first floor so he headed straight there and rapped on the door, steeling himself when she opened it. He could tell that she'd been crying but when he reached towards her, she stepped back.

'Yes? Did you want something?' she said in a voice that crackled with ice.

'I need to talk to you, Kelly, and find out if there's anything I can do to help. This is a very serious issue and it could have far-reaching consequences for your career.'

'And you think I don't know that?' She laughed harshly. 'If you were that worried about my career, Luca, you would have listened to what I was trying to tell you this morning.'

'So you still claim that you didn't write down that instruction on those notes?'

'I am not *claiming* anything. I wrote down the correct dosage and someone else altered it.' She stared back at him, her beautiful face set. 'It's up to you whether you believe me.'

He swore under his breath because she was putting him in an impossible position. 'I want to believe you, Kelly, but it was your signature on those notes.'

'And that means I'm guilty. If that's all, Luca, I think it's time you left, don't you?'

She started to close the door but he put out his hand and stopped her. 'Have you any proof of what you're saying?' he demanded.

'No. I don't have a shred of proof to back up my story but that doesn't mean it isn't true. The only proof I have is in here.' She placed her hand on her heart. 'I know I didn't make a mistake. I know what I wrote on Paolo's file and that what happened wasn't my fault. My heart knows the truth, Luca, but does yours?'

'Kelly, I…' he began desperately, but she shook her head.

'Don't waste your breath. I can tell that you think I'm lying. Goodnight, Luca.'

She closed the door and this time he didn't try to stop her. He felt too raw, too wounded by what she'd said to summon any resistance. Was she right? Should he have known in his heart whether or not she was to blame?

All his life he had found it difficult to trust people and he understood why. His mother had abandoned him, the people charged with his care had abused him, and nobody had given him any reason to believe in them. But it had been different when he'd met Kelly—he'd felt differently.

His head whirled as he went out to his car. He had trusted Kelly enough to open up his heart, trusted her enough to plan to spend his life with her. Not once had she betrayed his trust either, not when they were together two years ago and not since she had come back into his life now.

He was the one who had let *her* down. He had left her for another woman and it must have been a devastating experience for her. He hadn't told her the truth about Sophia and Matteo either. He had skirted over the facts, been less than honest with her, and now—to cap it all—he had refused to accept that she might be innocent of this error.

Guilt overwhelmed him when he realised how unfair he had been. He needed to reassess the situation and take what she'd said seriously. If someone had deliberately altered that file then he needed to find out who it was and deal with them before another tragedy occurred. And when that was done, he would tell Kelly the truth about him, Sophia and Matteo. Maybe it wouldn't make any difference to the eventual outcome, but she deserved to know why her life had been shattered two years ago. And maybe, just maybe, it would help to heal the wounds so that when she left Sardinia, she could put the whole unhappy episode behind her.

CHAPTER SEVENTEEN

THE following week was an absolute nightmare. With no job to go to, Kelly was left in a state of limbo. She tried to fill in the time as best she could, but she couldn't face the thought of having to see people and spent most of her time in the apartment.

What made it worse was that Luca didn't attempt to contact her again. It appeared that he had turned his back on her and it broke her heart to know that he believed she was guilty. She longed to tell Katie about what had happened, but whenever they spoke on the phone, Katie was bubbling with excitement about her upcoming wedding and Kelly didn't have the heart to ruin things for her.

Saturday arrived and she knew that she would go mad if she didn't go out. She deliberately chose a time when there would be few people about and booked a taxi to take her to the beach. It was crowded with holidaymakers but at least it meant that she was inconspicuous amongst the crowd.

She found a relatively quiet spot and laid out her towel. She'd brought a book with her so she settled down to read, realising after she'd read the same paragraph a dozen times that it was a waste of time. She couldn't concentrate with the threat of this inquiry hanging over her. If the panel didn't believe her story, she could find herself facing disciplinary action and she dreaded to imagine the effect that would have on her career.

Despair filled her at the thought of losing everything she had worked so hard to achieve. Abandoning the book, she decided to have a swim in the hope that it would clear her head. There were a lot of families with young children playing in the shallows close to the shore so she waded further out. She wasn't a particularly strong swimmer so she kept a careful watch on the shoreline to make sure she didn't go too far out. She was heading back when she heard a woman scream and looking round, she saw a child floating past her, clinging to a rubber dinghy.

Kelly didn't hesitate as she turned and swam after the dinghy. It was moving quite fast, caught up in one of the currents that swept around the bay. The little girl was stricken with terror as she was tossed about by the waves. A huge wave suddenly rolled towards the beach and Kelly's heart sank when she saw the dinghy being lifted into the air before it was plunged back into the water. She didn't need to hear the child's screams to know that she had lost her precarious hold.

Kelly swam as fast as she could, but the child had disappeared by the time she reached the dinghy. Taking a deep breath, she dived below the surface and saw the girl sinking towards the seabed. She knew that if she sank too deep she wouldn't be able to reach her so made one last frantic effort, and somehow managed to grab hold of her hair.

She swam back to the surface, hauling the child with her. The current was very strong this far out from shore and there was no hope of her swimming back to land when she would have to fight it. Rolling the child onto her back, she took a deep breath and blew into her mouth, relieved when the little girl immediately coughed up some water. Now all she needed to do was to keep them both afloat until help arrived.

It seemed to take for ever before anyone came to their aid. Several times Kelly found herself sinking and had to struggle to keep her head above the surface. When a speedboat arrived she could have wept with joy. A couple of men from the boat dived in and took the girl from her then helped her on board. Someone threw a blanket around her shoulders and she thanked them, but she was more concerned about the child. Although she was breathing, when salt water entered the lungs, it drew fluid into the alveoli—the tiny air sacs—from the vascular compartment. This not only damaged the lungs but could cause pulmonary oedema and hypoxia. Kelly was very aware that the child was still in danger.

'I'm a doctor,' she explained, crouching down beside the child. 'She will need to be admitted to hospital. It's imperative that she receives proper treatment.'

One of the men pulled out his mobile phone and dialled the emergency services. By the time they reached shore, Kelly could hear an ambulance siren in the distance. She scrambled out of the boat and told the men to lay the child on the sand. The girl's mother was beside herself with worry but she calmed down when Kelly explained that she was a doctor. She quickly checked the child over, frowning when she heard her struggling for breath. Water had definitely entered her lungs and it was essential that it be removed as quickly as possible.

'What's her name?' she asked the mother.

'Francesca.'

She rolled the little girl onto her side and bent over her. 'Francesca, I need you to cough up some more of that horrible water for me. I'm going to pat you on your back to see if that will help get rid of it.'

The child managed to nod so Kelly began patting her back and was relieved when Francesca vomited up some more sea water. She'd managed to get rid of it all by the time the ambulance arrived, but Kelly knew that she would need to be monitored very carefully on the way to the hospital.

'Will you go with her, *dottoressa?*' the child's mother pleaded. 'Something might happen on the way…' The poor woman couldn't continue, overcome by the thought of what might go wrong.

Kelly glanced at the lead paramedic. 'I'm happy to come if it's all right with you.'

The paramedic readily agreed and in a short time they were in the back of the ambulance. Kelly knelt beside the couch so she could keep an eye on the on-board monitoring equipment. Francesca's sats were down and the oxygen wasn't making a lot of difference. When the child suddenly arrested, Kelly immediately issued instructions to the other crew member.

'We need to shock her. I'll start CPR while you get everything ready.'

Bending over the child, she gave two inflations to her lungs then checked for any output. There was no pulse so she began chest compressions. As soon as the paramedic had the defibrillator ready, she took the paddles from him and applied them to the little girl's chest.

'Clear,' she instructed as she sent the electric current through the child's body. It did the trick and Francesca's heart immediately started beating again.

'Excellent.' Kelly handed back the paddles and replaced the oxygen mask. They had reached the hospital by then and she stood up, ready to help as soon as they stopped. The sooner the child was in Pronto Soccorso, the better her chances would be.

Kelly accompanied the stretcher into the building. Magdalena was waiting for them and she gasped when she saw Kelly. 'What are you doing here?'

'I happened to be at the beach when it happened so I lent a hand,' she explained, playing down her role.

'I'd say you did rather more than lend a hand,' Magdalena observed intuitively as they rushed the child to the resuscitation room.

Kelly shrugged, not wanting to be drawn on the subject when Francesca's life was hanging in the balance. She quickly explained what had happened on the journey there then left Magdalena to get on with her job. There was little else she could do to help so she made her way out of the emergency department, sighing when she remembered that she'd left all her belongings on the beach. Fortunately, she'd not had anything of value with her but it meant she would have to go back to collect her things after she got changed.

She had almost reached the main door when she saw a woman coming in and her heart sank when she realised it was Letizia. Letizia stopped when she saw her, her brows arching mockingly as she took in Kelly's bedraggled state.

'My, my, what have you been up to? It doesn't appear as though your enforced leave is doing you much good.'

'I'm really not interested in trading insults, Letizia,' she said shortly, attempting to pass her.

Letizia barred her way. 'You're not quite so clever now,

are you? It must have seemed like the perfect plan, too—sleep with Luca so he offers you the senior registrar's post. What a shame it didn't work.'

Kelly's blood ran cold as she stared at the other woman. 'I have no idea what you mean.'

Letizia laughed scornfully. 'Please, don't insult my intelligence by lying. I saw you leaving Luca's home the other morning. It was obvious what you'd been up to. I don't blame you either. I would have done exactly the same, given half the chance.'

'I did not sleep with Luca so he would offer me promotion,' Kelly enunciated very clearly. There was no point lying so she may as well tell the truth and be done with it. She stared at Letizia, seeing the disbelief on her face. 'I slept with him because I love him. It had nothing whatsoever to do with any job.'

Luca hadn't intended to go into work that day. Normally, he kept the weekends free so he could spend them with Matteo, but the worry over Kelly meant that he'd fallen behind with his work. As soon as Matteo went down for his afternoon nap, he left Maria in charge and drove to the hospital. A couple of hours in his office should clear the backlog and he would be able to start afresh on Monday morning.

He sighed as he stepped into the foyer. He was being optimistic if he thought the situation would be any easier by then. Knowing that he had hurt Kelly haunted him—he'd barely been able to function since the day she'd been suspended. He had tried to find out if anyone could have tampered with Paolo's file but it had proved to be an almost impossible task. Far too many people had handled the boy's notes and any one of them could have been the culprit. Without any proof, he couldn't accuse anyone of deliberately altering those figures.

Luca's heart was heavy as he made his way to the lifts. He didn't notice the two women standing to one side of the main door. It was only when he heard his name mentioned that he glanced round and felt his pulse quicken when he saw Kelly. He had no idea what had happened, but from the state of her, something was seriously wrong. He hurried towards her, only to come to an abrupt halt when he heard what she said. She had just told Letizia that she had slept with him because she loved him!

The blood rushed to his head, making it impossible to think. He could only stand as though rooted to the spot as Kelly hurried out of the building. Letizia looked furious as she swept past him, but he didn't care about her feelings—he only cared about Kelly. He had no idea what had prompted her to say that, but if it was true, and if Kelly did love him, then he needed to do something about it right now.

He raced out of the door but she had disappeared. Bearing in mind her state of dress, though, there could be only one place that she'd gone and that was her apartment. Luca made his way straight there, although his heart was pounding as he knocked on the door. What happened in the next few minutes could affect the rest of his life, yet all of a sudden every doubt he'd ever harboured suddenly disappeared. He could make this work, he was sure of it. He could give Kelly everything she needed. Please, heaven, that included him.

Kelly had just changed into a pair of linen trousers when she heard someone pounding on the door. For a moment she hesitated, unsure whether she should answer the summons.

If it was Letizia then she really didn't want to speak to her again. Why on earth had she blurted out that she loved Luca? It was bound to cause trouble, and she was in more than enough trouble as it was.

'Kelly, it's me. Open the door.'

She gasped when she recognised Luca's voice. She had no idea what he was doing here and wasn't sure if she wanted to speak to him after what had gone on the last time he'd paid her a visit. She made her way to the door although she didn't open it.

'I'm going out. I can't talk to you now, Luca.'

'It will only take a few minutes but I need to speak to you, Kelly,' he insisted. 'It's really important.'

He sounded so desperate that she found herself wavering.

'All right, but I can only spare you five minutes,' she said, opening the door.

'*Grazie,*' he murmured as he headed into the sitting room.

Kelly took a deep breath before she followed him. She had no idea what he wanted but she needed to keep control of her emotions if she wasn't to embarrass herself again that day. 'So what is it that you want to tell me, Luca?' she said coolly. 'Have you found out who altered those notes?'

'I'm afraid not. It isn't proving to be easy to pinpoint who was responsible for it.'

His deep voice grated and she shivered when she heard the strain it held. It took every scrap of willpower she could muster to maintain her composure. 'You make it sound as though you believe I'm innocent. You're not having second thoughts, are you?'

'Yes, I am, although I shouldn't have needed to think twice about it.' He took a step towards her and she could see the plea for forgiveness in his eyes. 'You were right, Kelly, I should have known in here that you were innocent of such a mistake.'

He placed his hand on his heart and Kelly realised that she couldn't hold out any longer. It had been the worst week of her life and to suddenly discover that Luca believed in her was too much to take in. Tears streamed down her face and she heard him groan.

'Don't, *cara*. Please, don't. I can't bear to see you crying and I know that I am responsible for it.'

He pulled her into his arms and cradled her against him, stroking her hair as he murmured soft words of comfort. Kelly clung to him as she sobbed out all her fear and pain. She wasn't sure how long they stayed like that. It was only when she heard someone knocking on the door that she lifted her head.

'If that's Letizia, I don't want to speak to her,' she whispered brokenly.

'Don't worry. I shall get rid of whoever it is,' he assured her as he went to the door.

Kelly sank down on the couch, feeling herself trembling from the aftermath of so much emotion. She had no idea what had made Luca change his mind, but that didn't matter nearly as much as the fact that he believed in her innocence. Her heart overflowed with happiness all of a sudden because she knew that she would find a way to prove that she hadn't been at fault now that she had his support.

'It was Aldo. He said that these belong to you. Apparently, you left them on the beach.'

Kelly gasped when she saw that he was holding her towel and bag. 'But how did Aldo know they were mine?'

'He said that he was there and saw what happened, how you swam after that little girl and saved her life.' Luca sat down beside her and took her hand so he could press a kiss to her palm. 'It appears everyone is talking about the brave and beautiful English doctor.'

Kelly blushed. 'I only did what anyone else would have done.'

'Oh, I doubt that, *cara*.' He pressed another tender kiss to her palm. 'There is only one Kelly Carlyon and she is a very special woman.'

Kelly shivered when she saw the warmth in his eyes. Even though it had been only a week since she had seen him look at her that way, she had missed him so much. She knew that they needed to clear up all the misunderstandings before they could resume their relationship—if that was what Luca wanted, of course.

Her breath caught at the thought of them being close again but she couldn't allow herself to get too carried away just yet. 'I never made a mistake about that insulin, Luca. I know I didn't even if I can't prove it. Someone altered the figures and left me to take the blame.'

'And we shall find out who did it and make sure they are punished,' he said quietly.

'So you really do believe me?' she whispered, her eyes welling up with tears once again.

'Yes. I don't know why I ever doubted you.' He gripped her hands. 'I suppose it was because I find it so difficult to trust people.'

'Because of the way your mother abandoned you?'

'Yes.' He sighed. 'It isn't difficult to understand why I feel like this, is it? I learned at a young age that people weren't to be trusted and that has stayed with me all my life. I was abused when I lived at the children's home, all the children were, and it coloured my view of life.'

'Abused?' she echoed in horror. 'You don't mean sexually?'

'No. At least that is something to be grateful for. The abuse we suffered was more psychological than anything else. Oh, there were the odd beatings, but it was the lack of love we were shown and the fact that we were told repeatedly that we were worthless that did the most damage. Every child in that home was left with scars, myself included.'

'Oh, Luca, I'm so sorry. I had no idea.' She gripped his hands, wanting in some way to let him know that she cared about what had happened to him even if she could never make up for it.

'*Grazie, cara.* It means a lot to me to hear you say that. It's far more than I deserve, bearing in mind what I did to you.'

He paused and she had a feeling that he was steeling himself before he told her something even more important. Although she had no idea what it was, she knew it wouldn't make any difference to the way she felt about him. She loved him with all her heart and nothing that had happened in his past would alter that.

'Sophia was in the home with me, although her circumstances were somewhat different to mine. Her parents had been killed in an automobile accident and as she had no other family, she was sent to the home. She was very quiet and shy, and the other children bullied her until I made them leave her alone. After that, we were inseparable.'

'You must have shared an awful lot,' Kelly said softly, hating herself for feeling jealous of their closeness.

'We did. It's impossible to explain it, Kelly. You would have had to be there to understand how desperate we were for any kind of emotional support.' He took a steadying breath, overcome by the memory of those dark days. 'Sophia was my only friend, the only person I cared about in those days.'

'And you two continued to care about each other after you grew up?'

'*Si.*' He looked at her and she saw the determination in his eyes. 'I would have done anything to protect Sophia, and that included marrying her.'

'I'm not sure I understand,' Kelly said slowly. 'Surely you married her because you loved her? After all, she was expecting your child.'

'No, she wasn't.' He looked straight into her eyes. 'I am not Matteo's father.'

CHAPTER EIGHTEEN

'Not his father...? What do you mean? I don't understand.'

Luca felt the blood drum through his veins when he heard the shock in her voice. Maybe he should have broken the news to her some other way instead of blurting it out, but now that he had come this far he had to go on. He stood up and paced the floor, unable to sit still while he explained everything to her.

'Matteo isn't my biological child. Sophia had an affair with a married man. When she told him that she was pregnant, he broke off the relationship. She never heard from him again.'

'And you knew about this when you married her? You knew the baby wasn't yours?'

'Of course.' He stopped in front of the couch, feeling worse than ever when he saw how pale she looked. 'Sophia and I were never lovers, *cara*. We were like brother and sister, it would have been unthinkable for us to have had an intimate relationship.'

'I see,' she said slowly, obviously struggling to take it all in. 'So why did you marry her, then?'

'Because she begged me to for the sake of her child.'

He sank down onto the seat, although he didn't take hold

of her hands again. He needed to let her decide what she wanted to do, whether or not she wanted to be with him. He hurried on because he couldn't bear to imagine what might happen after he finished his tale.

'Sophia knew it was unlikely that she would live long enough to see her child grow up. She was desperate to ensure that the baby wasn't sent to a home like the one we'd been in. She asked me if I would marry her so that my name could go on the birth certificate and there would never be any question of Matteo being taken into care.'

'Is that why you married her so soon after you returned to Italy?'

'*Si*. I didn't want her worrying about what would happen to her child when she was so ill.'

'Why didn't you tell me this before?'

'Because she made me promise that I would keep it a secret,' he said simply. 'She was terrified that the authorities would find out and take Matteo away from me.'

'But you've told me now,' she pointed out.

'Yes, because I want you to know the truth, Kelly. I trust you, *cara*. I know that you would never do anything to harm Matteo.'

'Thank you,' she whispered, her voice breaking when she realised how much it had cost him to share this secret with her. Trust had been lacking in his life, yet he trusted her and she couldn't begin to explain how much it meant to her.

She captured his hands and held them tightly. 'I swear on my life that I will never tell anyone what you have just told me, Luca.'

'I know you won't.' He smiled at her, a smile that was filled with such tenderness that she couldn't help herself. Leaning forward, she kissed him on the mouth, letting him know how much that simple statement had meant to her.

'Will you tell Matteo the truth when he's old enough to understand?' she asked, drawing back before she gave in to the urge to stay in his arms and never leave them. Although Luca had opened his heart to her, there was no reason to believe he had changed his mind about them.

'Yes. It's what Sophia wanted and I believe it's the right thing to do, too. She wrote him a letter, explaining everything, so that will help. And, hopefully, he will be secure enough by then to cope with the news.'

'He will be fine as long as he has you, Luca. No child could want a better father than you.'

'Thank you.' He smiled at her again, although she sensed there was something else he wanted to tell her. She was already steeling herself when he continued. 'It means an awful lot to me to hear you say that, Kelly. I thought that after what happened between us you would never be able to forgive me.'

'Now that I understand why you did what you did, of course I forgive you. You had no choice, Luca. You also wouldn't be the man I thought you were if you'd let Sophia go through such a terrible ordeal on her own.'

'So I do have some good points?' he said in a teasing tone, although his eyes told a very different story about how he was feeling.

'I…um, yes, of course you do,' she said quickly. She went to stand up, suddenly uncertain where the conversation was leading, but he wouldn't let her go.

'Enough good points that you might still care about me?'

'Yes.' It came out as a strangled gasp but this wasn't easy

for her. If she told him the truth, that she loved him, he might not want to hear it.

'I care about you too, *cara*.' He pulled her to him and kissed her softly on the mouth. 'I love you, Kelly. I have never stopped loving you, in fact.'

'You love me?'

'*Si*. And I think you might feel the same way about me.'

He paused, leaving the question hanging in the air. Kelly could feel her heart racing, but there was really only one answer she could give him.

'I love you, too, Luca. I thought I'd got over you but I realised when I saw you again that I hadn't. And now that I understand why you left me, I love you even more.'

'*Cara.*' He swept her into his arms and held her tightly against him. 'I adore you. I want nothing more than to spend the rest of my life with you.'

Kelly laughed. 'That's how I feel as well. How come we've never admitted it before?'

'Because I was terrified that I would ruin your life if I told you how I felt.' His expression was very grave as he set her away from him. 'I know how important your career is to you, Kelly, and I would hate to be responsible for damaging it.'

'How on earth could you do that?' she said in genuine bewilderment.

'You must know how difficult it is for a woman to reach the top even in these so-called enlightened times. And a woman who has a family...' He broke off and sighed.

'So you thought it would be better if you kept me at arm's length?' she guessed.

'It seemed the only way to protect you. I love you too

much to want to hurt you again. If that meant sending you away, that's what I was prepared to do.'

'And what if I told you that it's a risk I'm prepared to take, that my career might be important to me but it's not as important as how I feel about you?' she said softly, cradling his face between her hands.

'First I would turn cartwheels for joy and then I would worry in case you were making a mistake.' He turned his head, letting the tip of his tongue stroke her palm in a caress that sent a flood of desire coursing through her. 'I couldn't bear it if you ended up hating me for ruining your life, my darling. It would destroy me.'

'I would never, ever, blame you, Luca,' she said firmly. 'I'm old enough to know what I want out of life, and if I choose to be with you and put my career on hold, it will be my decision.'

'But you are a very talented doctor,' he protested. 'You could reach the very top of the professional ladder without any hindrances.'

'I don't see love as a hindrance. I see it as blessing, a rare and beautiful gift.' She kissed him on the mouth then smiled into his eyes. 'Let me show you how much I love you and then we can decide what we're going to do.'

Luca needed no further persuasion. He pulled her into his arms and kissed her with a passion that had her clinging to him. They made love right there in the sitting room with the afternoon sun gilding their naked bodies, and after it was over, Kelly knew that she had made the right decision, the only decision. She loved her job and wanted to succeed, but Luca meant more to her than her career. He was her whole world, her life, him and Matteo.

She told him that as they lay sleepily in one another's arms, sated by passion, and he cried, tears of joy and relief which helped to heal some of the pain he had suffered. Kelly held him and stroked his hair, knowing that he couldn't have shown her in any other way how much she meant to him. He had torn down all the barriers and now she was on the inside instead of being kept on the outside.

It was a moment of such profundity that she knew she would remember if for the rest of her life. She also knew that she would never do anything to damage his trust in her. As they drifted off to sleep in her bed a short time later, she felt a sense of completeness which had been missing before. She had Luca to care for and love; he had her to care for and love in return. Their lives were melding into one beautiful whole.

EPILOGUE

'LUCA, stop it! The taxi is going to be here soon and I still haven't finished packing.'

Kelly managed to break free but Luca simply grabbed hold of her again, and dropped another kiss on her lips. 'If we miss the plane then we shall catch a later flight,' he growled.

'And how do I explain to my sister why we missed the plane?' she demanded as he pressed her back against the pillows. She wasn't really annoyed with him, of course. After only a month together she was more than happy to spend as long as possible in his arms. But she felt that she should make a token protest otherwise he would think he could have everything his own way after they were married.

A shiver rippled through her at the thought of their wedding. She and Katie had decided to have a double wedding in Cyprus. After the ceremony, she, Luca and Matteo would spend their honeymoon at Christos's villa in Paphos while Katie and Christos flew to Sardinia to spend their honeymoon here. It was the perfect arrangement and she was looking forward to it immensely. Mind you, she looked forward to every day now that she and Luca were together.

'I don't think your sister will need it explained to her,' Luca assured her. 'She is in love and she understands these things.' He kissed her again, a lingering kiss that stole her breath as well as her ability to worry about travel arrangements.

She wound her arms around his neck and sighed. 'Do you think we will ever get tired of making love?'

'No. We will still feel the same when we are a hundred,' he told her with a wicked little chuckle.

'If we can still manage this when we're a hundred, we'll be in all the record books,' she retorted. She kissed him again then wriggled out of his arms. 'I have to finish packing. Promise me that you will be good and not keep distracting me.'

He folded his arms across his bare chest and leered at her. 'I'll try.'

'I suppose that will have to do,' she grumbled as she busied herself stowing underwear into her case. The most important item, her wedding dress, had been packed already but she couldn't resist unzipping the garment bag and taking another peek.

It was the most glorious confection of antique lace with a full skirt and a sweeping train. Maria had insisted on lending her the veil she had worn at her own wedding and that was carefully packed in tissue paper and tucked into the back of the bag. Kelly had felt like a princess when she had tried it on after the final fitting and couldn't wait to wear it for her wedding in two days' time. However, before she reached that high point, she needed to finish packing.

She bustled about and soon had everything laid out on the bed. Fortunately, she'd helped Matteo pack the night before so she didn't have to worry about that. The little boy didn't really understand what was happening but he was very excited at the thought of them going away on holiday. He seemed to have accepted that she was part of his life now and she in turn had grown to love him. She knew that when she and Luca had a family of their own, her feelings wouldn't change. Matteo was a very special little boy and she would do everything she could to make sure that Sophia's son grew up knowing how much he was loved and wanted.

'I think that's it… Oh, no, I almost forgot my shoes.' Dashing across the bedroom, she hauled out the shoe box from under the chest of drawers and tried to squeeze it into her suitcase. 'It won't fit,' she declared in dismay.

'Here, let me have it.' Luca got out of bed and took the box from her, stowing it neatly away in his own case. 'There. Is that everything now?'

'I think so,' Kelly replied, somewhat distracted by the sight of his naked body.

'I thought we needed to hurry up,' he said, grinning as he pulled her into his arms.

'Mmm, we do,' she murmured, then shrieked in horror when she heard the doorbell ring. 'Oh, that can't be the taxi already.'

Luca let her go and went to the window. 'It's the post van. I'll see what he wants.'

'And I'll go and take a shower before the taxi gets here,' Kelly informed him with a sigh.

Luca was sitting on the bed when she went back into the room and she frowned when she saw that he was holding a letter. 'What's that?'

'It's for you from the board of inquiry. They promised that they would let you have their decision as soon as possible.'

Kelly's heart plummeted. With all the preparations for the wedding, she'd not given much thought to the outcome of the inquiry, although, in the event, it had been less traumatic than she'd feared. After she had told Luca her suspicions about Letizia he had made some enquiries and discovered that Letizia had been seen with Paolo's notes shortly before the boy had been given his morning injection of insulin. It had been too much of a coincidence, especially allied to what else they had discovered.

Apparently, there had been a similar incident at the hospital where Letizia had worked prior to moving to Sardinia. No blame had been attached to her, which was why there'd been no mention of it in her references.

Luca had interviewed her and while she hadn't admitted what she'd done, she'd said enough to convince him that she was to blame. He had given her a choice: either she resigned or she would face an inquiry and be dismissed.

She had taken the first option and had left, proving conclusively to everyone that she was guilty. Although it had been a relief to know that her colleagues had no longer blamed her for what had happened, Kelly had been worried in case the board of inquiry had needed further proof, so her hands were shaking as she ripped open the envelope.

'Well?' Luca said impatiently. 'What does it say?'

'They've exonerated me.' She smiled in delight. 'It says here that "no blame has been attached to my name for the incident in question". That seems pretty conclusive, doesn't it?'

'It certainly does.' He pulled her to him and kissed her lingeringly. 'And to think I ever doubted you. Can you ever forgive me, *cara*?'

'Hmm, maybe. You might need to perform a few really tough penances, though,' she said, smiling at him.

'Really? What sort of penances do you have in mind?' he growled, smoothing his hand down her back.

'I'll have to think about that,' she whispered, feeling her breath catch as his hand gently cupped her bottom.

'And while you're dreaming up a suitable punishment, I'll fill in the time, shall I?'

He swept her into his arms and carried her back to the bed, kissing her hungrily as he laid her down on the rumpled sheets. Kelly kissed him back then wound her arms around his neck and pulled him down to lie beside her.

'It could take me some time to think up a suitable penance for you,' she warned him.

'Good.' He kissed her again, stroking his palms over her breasts and smiling when he felt her nipples peak. 'The more time the better.'

Kelly closed her eyes and let herself drift away on a sea of passion, only to be rudely interrupted by the sound of a car horn being blown outside the window. 'The taxi!' she exclaimed, attempting to sit up.

Luca pressed her back against the pillows. 'I'll tell the driver to come back later when we aren't so busy.'

'But what about our flight?'

'I'll book us on another one.' He kissed her again. 'Don't worry, *cara*, we won't miss our wedding. We will get to Cyprus in time for you to walk down the aisle, but some things are more important than a missed flight. Some things can't wait, and showing you how much I love you is top of my list.'

'I love you, too,' she whispered.

She closed her eyes as he left the room, anticipating the moment when he would come back to her. He was right because there was nothing more important than their love. They had come so close to losing one another that every second they spent together was even more precious.

Her mind drifted forward to the moment when she would make her vows. From that moment on, she and Luca would never be apart again.

FREE!

4 Books
and a surprise gift!

We would like to take this opportunity to thank you for reading this Mills & Boon® book by offering you the chance to take FOUR more specially selected titles from the Medical™ series absolutely FREE! We're also making this offer to introduce you to the benefits of the Mills & Boon® Reader Service™—

- ★ FREE home delivery
- ★ FREE gifts and competitions
- ★ FREE monthly Newsletter
- ★ Exclusive Reader Service offers
- ★ Books available before they're in the shops

Accepting these FREE books and gift places you under no obligation to buy, you may cancel at any time, even after receiving your free shipment. Simply complete your details below and return the entire page to the address below. You don't even need a stamp!

YES! Please send me 4 free Medical books and a surprise gift. I understand that unless you hear from me, I will receive 6 superb new titles every month for just £2.89 each, postage and packing free. I am under no obligation to purchase any books and may cancel my subscription at any time. The free books and gift will be mine to keep in any case.

M7ZEF

Ms/Mrs/Miss/Mr ....Initials...............................
BLOCK CAPITALS PLEASE

Surname ....

Address ....

....

....Postcode....................................

Send this whole page to:
UK: FREEPOST CN81, Croydon, CR9 3WZ

Offer valid in UK only and is not available to current Mills & Boon® Reader Service™ subscribers to this series. Overseas and Eire please write for details. We reserve the right to refuse an application and applicants must be aged 18 years or over. Only one application per household. Terms and prices subject to change without notice. Offer expires 30th November 2007. As a result of this application, you may receive offers from Harlequin Mills & Boon and other carefully selected companies. If you would prefer not to share in this opportunity please write to The Data Manager, PO Box 676, Richmond, TW9 IWU.

Mills & Boon® is a registered trademark owned by Harlequin Mills & Boon Limited.
Medical™ is being used as a trademark. The Mills & Boon® Reader Service™ is being used as a trademark.